'I can't,' she admitted. 'I can't explain what I was doing on that plane. I suppose it's possible we'll never know, but if I'm to stay here—'

'There's no question of anything other,' came the harsh interruption.

Karen spread her hands. 'Fine. I accept that. Only we both have to make the effort to put things right between us. If you turn me down now...'

'You think me capable of it?' He threw back the sheet, revealing his nudity all the way down. He was already fully and heart-jerkingly aroused. Karen felt her stomach muscles contract, the heat rush through her.

'You're right,' he said on a softer note. 'Our only recourse is to wipe the past from mind. Come.'

Heart thudding like a hammer, every nerve ending in her body on fire. she reached the bed.

He said something words foreign to understandable. W her, she went willin

Kay Thorpe was born in Sheffield in 1935. She tried out a variety of jobs after leaving school. Writing began as a hobby, becoming a way of life only after she had her first completed novel accepted for publication in 1968. Since then she's written over fifty, and lives now with her husband, son, German Shepherd dog and lucky black cat on the outskirts of Chesterfield in Derbyshire. Her interests include reading, hiking and travel.

Recent titles by the same author:

MOTHER AND MISTRESS
MISTRESS TO A BACHELOR

THE SOUTH AMERICAN'S WIFE

BY

KAY THORPE

DID YOU PURCHASE THIS BOOK WITHOUT A COVER?

If you did, you should be aware it is **stolen property** as it was reported *unsold and destroyed* by a retailer. Neither the author nor the publisher has received any payment for this book.

All the characters in this book have no existence outside the imagination of the author, and have no relation whatsoever to anyone bearing the same name or names. They are not even distantly inspired by any individual known or unknown to the author, and all the incidents are pure invention.

All Rights Reserved including the right of reproduction in whole or in part in any form. This edition is published by arrangement with Harlequin Enterprises II B.V. The text of this publication or any part thereof may not be reproduced or transmitted in any form or by any means, electronic or mechanical, including photocopying, recording, storage in an information retrieval system, or otherwise, without the written permission of the publisher.

This book is sold subject to the condition that it shall not, by way of trade or otherwise, be lent, resold, hired out or otherwise circulated without the prior consent of the publisher in any form of binding or cover other than that in which it is published and without a similar condition including this condition being imposed on the subsequent purchaser.

MILLS & BOON and MILLS & BOON with the Rose Device are registered trademarks of the publisher.

First published in Great Britain 2004
Harlequin Mills & Boon Limited,
Eton House, 18-24 Paradise Road, Richmond, Surrey TW9 1SR

© Kay Thorpe 2004

ISBN 0 263 83739 4

Set in Times Roman 10½ on 12 pt.
01-0504-47193

Printed and bound in Spain
by Litografia Rosés, S.A., Barcelona

CHAPTER ONE

SOFT but insistent, the sound of her name drew Karen out of a dreamless sleep. She opened her eyes to gaze for a blank moment or two at the unfamiliar, sun-filled room, her mind struggling to orientate itself.

Her eyes dropped to the lean, brown masculine hand covering hers where it lay on the white bed cover, travelling slowly up the length of a bronzed muscular arm to reach the face of the man seated at the bedside: a vital masculine face beneath thick black hair, short-cropped to control its curl.

'So you're back with us at last,' he said in heavily accented English.

Mind still fogged, Karen eyed him in perplexity. 'I don't understand,' she murmured, surprised to hear how weak her voice sounded. 'What happened? Where am I?'

Some nameless expression flickered across the dark eyes. 'You were involved in an accident and suffered a concussion,' he said. 'You're in hospital here in Rio.'

The fog deepened. 'Rio?'

'Rio de Janeiro.' He paused, brows drawing together. 'Do you not remember?'

Karen stared at him in total confusion. Rio de Janeiro? That was in Brazil, wasn't it? The farthest she'd ever been from home was Spain!

'I don't understand,' she repeated helplessly. 'Who are you?'

There was no immediate answer; the expression on the hard-boned face was disturbing. When he did speak it was in measured tones. 'I'm Luiz Andrade. Your husband.'

She froze, eyes wide and dark, mind whirling. 'I don't have a husband,' she got out. 'What kind of game is this?'

The hand still covering hers tightened as she tried to draw it away. 'The concussion has confused you. Relax, and everything will come back to you.'

'No, it won't, because it isn't true!' She pressed herself upright, wincing as pain shot through her head, but in no frame of mind to give way to it. 'I'm Karen Downing! I live in London! I've never been to Rio de Janeiro in my life, and I'm certainly not married—to you or anyone!'

'Hush! You must not agitate yourself this way.' Looking concerned, he reached for the bell-push on the bedside table. 'The doctor will give you something to calm you. When you waken, everything will be clear again.'

'No!' She tore her hand free, shrinking as far as she could get from this stranger, now on his feet and towering over her. 'It's all lies!'

'Why would I lie?' he asked. 'For what possible reason would I claim to be your husband if it were not the truth?'

'I don't know!' she flung back. 'All I do know is that I never saw you before in my life!'

As if on cue, the door opened to admit a uniformed nurse. Looking from one to the other, she said something in a language totally foreign to Karen's ears, answered by the man claiming to be her husband in what appeared to be the same language.

'What did you tell her?' she demanded as the woman exited again.

'To fetch a doctor,' he said. 'You're obviously suffering from a temporary amnesia.'

'There's nothing temporary about it!' she claimed. 'Whatever this is about, you can forget it!' She glanced down at the white hospital smock she was wearing, then wildly about her. 'Where are my clothes?'

'The ones you were wearing at the time of the accident have been disposed of,' he said. 'Others will be brought when you're deemed fit to be discharged.'

'I want to go now!' she shot back at him. 'You can't keep me here against my will.'

Powerful shoulders lifted. 'To where would you go? You know no one in Rio.' A muscle jerked in the firm jawline as if he'd clamped his teeth together on some addition to that statement. 'Be patient,' he went on after a moment, 'and everything will be all right.'

He turned as the door opened again, this time to admit a white-coated doctor, addressing him in the same language he'd used with the nurse. Portuguese was the language spoken in Brazil; Karen knew that for a fact. She felt trapped in a never-ending nightmare.

The fight went out of her suddenly. She subsided on to the bed, unable to summon the strength of either mind or body to protest when the doctor produced a syringe. Sleep would be a welcome release from the turmoil in her head.

She opened her eyes again to soft lamplight, and for a moment imagined herself safe in her own bedroom, having fallen asleep reading as she often did.

Only it wasn't her room, and it hadn't been a dream, because the same man was seated at the bedside.

'How are you feeling now?' he asked.

Her voice came out low and ragged. 'Afraid.'

Face expressionless, he said, 'Do you know me?'

Karen shook her head, too demoralised by the realisation that the nightmare hadn't ended to summon any semblance of spirit.

'So what exactly *do* you remember?' he asked.

'I'm Karen Downing,' she said. 'I'm twenty-three years old, and I share a flat in London with a friend who works for the same firm. My parents were killed in a plane crash four years ago.'

That memory alone was enough to pierce her fragile control. She swallowed on the lump in her throat, recalling the agony of those days, weeks, months it had taken her to come to terms with her loss.

'This much I already know,' Luiz Andrade returned. 'What appears to have happened is that your mind has somehow blanked out the past three months of your life. The three months you've spent here in Brazil as my wife.' He paused again, as if gathering himself. 'We met at the hotel where you were spending a holiday. We were married within the week.'

'That's impossible!' Karen burst out. 'I'd never...'

She broke off, biting her lip. If she couldn't remember, how could she be sure of *what* she might have done? But three months! Three whole months missing from her life! It didn't seem possible!

'How did I get to Rio?' she asked, forcing herself to calm down a little. 'I couldn't afford a holiday in Brazil on my earnings.'

'You told me you had won a sum of money on your

lottery, and decided to see something of the world outside of Europe while you had the opportunity.'

'So you didn't marry me on the assumption that I was rich,' she murmured, trying to make sense of the story.

The strong, sensual mouth slanted briefly. 'It was your beauty that attracted my eye, your personality that captured my heart.' He registered the expression that crossed her face with another humourless smile. 'You looked much the same way the first time I made my feelings clear to you—as if you doubted your power to stir a man to such a degree. Only when we made love did you begin to believe in me.'

Warmth rose beneath her skin as her eyes dropped involuntarily down the length of his body to the lean hips and long legs clad in close-fitting white jeans, the stirring deep down in the pit of her stomach no fluke of imagination.

'You were a virgin,' he went on softly. 'That in itself would have been enough to seal my fate. It was fortunate that you felt for me too, because I would not easily have let you go.'

It had to be true, Karen thought desperately. As he'd said before, what possible reason could he have to lie? If only she could find even the slightest kink in the blanket cloaking her mind!

'You said we were married within a week of meeting?' she ventured.

'Just five days, to be precise. For me, it would have been sooner, but there were necessary formalities to be observed. We travelled to my home in São Paulo the following day.'

Karen's brows were drawn in the effort to recall,

but there wasn't even a glimmer. 'You're saying I never went back home at all?'

'There seemed no need when you had so little to return for. Your friend was contacted, and your place of work.'

'But my things!'

'Most of which you had with you. The apartment apparently was rented. The few items you did express a desire to have were despatched by your friend.'

Karen absorbed the information in silence for a moment, trying to imagine Julie's reaction to the news. 'It must have been a tremendous shock for her,' she said at length.

'I imagine it was. You're still in touch with her, if you feel the ring you wear isn't verification enough.'

Karen raised her hand slowly to gaze at the wide gold band, shaking her head in numb acceptance. 'I believe you. I *have* to believe you! It's just so difficult to take in.'

'It must be.' Luiz leaned forward to ease his position, lips twisting as she flinched. 'You have nothing to fear. Retribution is farthest from my mind.'

Karen felt her heart jerk. 'Retribution?' she got out. 'For what?'

It was apparent from the expression in the dark eyes that he regretted having said what he had. 'There are matters perhaps best left alone for the present,' he declared. 'The problems are many already without adding to them.'

'I want to know what you meant,' she insisted, every nerve in her body on edge. 'I have a right to know!'

The hesitation was brief, the lift of his shoulders signifying resignation. 'Very well. You came to Rio in the company of a man named Lucio Fernandas, with whom you had apparently been carrying on an affair. I followed you in order to bring you back, but the accident happened before I even reached the city. Perhaps fortunately,' he added on a harder note, 'or I may have been driven to measures that would have done none of us any good.'

Karen had difficulty finding any words at all. An affair? She'd been having an affair!

'Are you sure?' she asked faintly.

The firm mouth acquired a cynical slant. 'Why else would you have run away with the man?'

'I don't know,' she admitted. And then with a flash of spirit, 'But if it is true, why on earth would you have wanted me back?'

'What is mine remains mine.' The statement was all the more compelling for its lack of force. 'There has never been, nor ever will be, a divorce in the Andrade family—no matter what the provocation.'

Karen felt a sudden shiver run down her spine. She made a valiant effort to regain control of herself.

'So where is he, this Lucio Fernandas?'

'Vanished, like the coward he is!' The contempt was searing. 'You were alone when the medics reached you.'

'Reached me where?'

'At the road outside the airport where you were hit by a car. It was fortunate that your bag wasn't stolen while you lay unconscious. Once your identity was proven, news was relayed to our home, then passed to me on landing.' His jaw contracted. 'You were unconscious for almost two hours. It was feared that your skull was fractured.'

Karen considered the foregoing, feeling ever more

confused. 'You said the news was passed to you on landing?'

'I set out after you the moment I became aware of your departure this morning,' Luiz acknowledged. 'You'd taken your passport, but I doubted that you would have gone straight to the international airport in case of pursuit. I was right. Unfortunately, I was fifteen minutes too late to catch you at Congonhas. I took the next flight to Rio. Having first checked that Fernandas was on the plane too,' he added, anticipating the question hovering on her lips. 'There was no mistake.'

'I'm…sorry.' It was totally inadequate, but all she could come up with for the moment.

The dark head inclined. 'I'm the one who should be sorry. I shouldn't have told you all this so soon.' He got to his feet, body lithe as a panther's. 'You must rest. I'll see you again in the morning.'

Stranger or not, she didn't want him to go. At least while he was here she could keep on asking the questions crowding her mind—keep on hoping for that breakthrough.

'I can't stay here!' she exclaimed on a note of desperation.

'You have to stay.' His tone brooked no argument. 'At least until we can be sure you suffered no deeper damage. Perhaps a night's sleep will restore you.'

He didn't believe that any more than she did, Karen reckoned. Whatever the reason for her memory loss, it was going to take more than a night's sleep to restore it. In the meantime, she had no other recourse but to do as he said.

Thankfully, he made no attempt to touch her in any way, but simply lifted a hand in farewell. She watched him go to the door, appraising the tapering line from broad shoulder to narrow waist and hip. A fine figure of a man in any language. She had lain in his arms, known the intimate intrusion of his body. How could any woman forget that? How could any woman forget *him*?

The nurse who came in after he'd gone was different from the one before, but kindness itself. She insisted on helping Karen across to the *en suite* bathroom. A welcome hand, Karen found when she stood up.

There was a full length mirror on the back of the bathroom door. The face looking back at her was pale, throwing into sharp contrast the purpling bruise at the temple. The wide-spaced green eyes looked bruised too, the soft, full mouth vulnerable. There was some grazing across cheek and jawline, though superficial enough to make any scarring unlikely.

If nothing else had convinced her of the passage of time, the couple of inches her hair had grown since she last recalled looking at it would have done so. Natural silver-blonde in colour, it fell curtain straight to her shoulders.

Luiz would be in his early thirties, she calculated. The kind of man most women would find devastatingly attractive, she had to acknowledge. She could well imagine the impact he would have had on her at first sight: an impact deep enough to make her willing to give up everything she'd ever known just to be with him.

Which made the idea of her having had an affair with another man within three months of marrying him even harder to believe.

The nurse waiting outside knocked on the door. 'You are well?' she called.

Karen gathered herself together. There was nothing to be gained from standing here grappling with matters she had no knowledge of. All she could hope for was eventual enlightenment.

A sleeping pill gave her a good night's rest, but morning brought no change. Awake at five-thirty, with little of yesterday's physical unsteadiness left, she got up to take a shower and wash her hair. She had no make-up to hand, and nothing but the gown left by last night's nurse to put on, but at least she felt bodily refreshed.

Where she went from here she had no clear idea. She was married to a man she not only didn't remember, but whose trust she had apparently betrayed. Even if he was prepared to take her back, could she bear to go with him?

Yet what other choice did she have when it came right down to it? She had neither home nor job to return to in England, even if she still had the means left to get there.

Back in the bedroom, she drew the window blind to look out on a picture postcard view of sparkling white skyscrapers and green parks stretching down to a sea the same deep blue as the great bowl of sky above it. Rising from a jutting peninsula, the conical shape of Sugar Loaf Mountain was recognisable from a multitude of travelogues.

Built up here in the foothills of the backing mountains, this was no common or garden hospital, Karen realised—something she should have known already from the standard of both furnishings and facilities. Luiz Andrade was obviously a man of some means.

She dismissed the idea that that might have had something to do with her readiness to marry him. If the very thought of it turned her stomach now, it would certainly have done the same then.

Breakfast was brought by yet another nurse, who spoke no English at all. Karen picked at the fruit and cereal, mind still going around in circles. Physically she was surely well enough to leave the hospital today, which made it imperative that she come to terms with her predicament.

Luiz Andrade was her husband. That much she had to accept. What concerned her the most at present was what he might expect from her. She had no idea of a wife's rights here. For all she knew, he could be within his in demanding an immediate resumption of marital relations, regardless of her condition. There had been an element of ruthlessness about him last night when he'd spoken of what he might have done had he caught up with her missing lover. It wasn't beyond the realms of possibility that she might have suffered some form of retribution herself before being dragged back to wherever it was that they lived.

She was in a state bordering on panic by the time Luiz put in an appearance. He was wearing the same white jeans and shirt—both items freshly washed and pressed from the look of it.

'I brought no change of clothing,' he said, correctly interpreting the unspoken question. 'There was no time. The hotel where I spent the night provides laundry facilities.' He studied her, dark eyes revealing nothing of his thoughts. 'How do you feel now?'

'Much the same,' she acknowledged, fighting the

urge to throw a wobbly. 'Mentally, at any rate. Physically, I don't think there's a great deal wrong with me.'

'We'll allow the doctors to decide that.' He moved to take a seat on the edge of the bed itself, registering her involuntary movement with a narrowing of his lips. 'You certainly look more yourself this morning. Apart from the bruising, of course. Is your head very painful still?'

'Only if I move it too sharply.' Karen was doing her best to maintain a stiff upper lip, vitally aware of the warmth radiating from the well-honed body. 'I'd feel a whole world better for a touch of lipstick!'

'You have no need of cosmetics to enhance your looks,' he declared. 'Your hair alone is colour enough.'

'I washed it,' she said, desperate to keep the conversation on an inconsequential level. 'It was filthy.'

'Hardly surprising after being dragged in the dust.' Luiz put up a hand to tuck a still damp strand back from her cheek, refusing this time to be put off by her jerky movement. 'Is my touch so obnoxious to you?'

'It's an automatic reflex,' she said. 'Nothing personal. I just can't get my head round this whole situation.'

'I find it difficult myself,' he admitted. 'You gave no indication that you no longer found my attentions desirable. Our lovemaking the very night before you left was—'

'Don't!' Karen was trembling, the muscle spasm high in her inner thighs a hint that her body might remember what her mind did not. 'Can't we talk about something else?'

'What would you suggest?' he asked drily.

She cast around. 'Your home?'

'*Our* home,' Luiz corrected. 'The home to which we shall be returning.' He shifted from the bed to the chair he had occupied the night before, face expressionless again. 'São Paulo is many kilometres from here, the city the largest in Brazil, the state one of the richest. Guavada is a cattle ranch lying to the north-west of the city.

Nothing of what he was telling her meant anything. A cattle ranch!

'You're a manager or something?' she hazarded.

About to answer, Luiz broke off as the door opened to admit the same white-coated doctor from the night before, getting to his feet to greet the man.

The latter came to examine the bruise on Karen's temple, shining a torch into each eye before finally pronouncing himself satisfied with her condition.

'You are fortunate,' he said, 'that the damage was no worse.'

'I don't see amnesia as a light matter,' she retorted. 'Have you any idea how long it might last?'

The man hesitated, obviously reluctant to commit himself to a prognosis. 'Your memory could return at any time,' he said at length. 'Shock can do many things to the mind. You must be patient and try not to worry about it.'

Easy enough to say, Karen reflected hollowly. How could she *not* worry about it?

Luiz walked with the man to the door, returning to announce that she was cleared to leave the hospital.

'Your bag will be brought for you to select fresh clothing,' he said. 'Shall you need help in dressing?'

'No!' The denial came out sharper than she had intended, drawing another of the cynical smiles.

'I was thinking of a nurse's assistance, not my own.'

'I'm sorry.' She made a helpless little gesture. 'It isn't that I don't trust you.'

'Is it not?' he asked softly. 'Can you truly claim to believe that every word I've spoken is the truth?'

'I have to believe it,' she said. 'I don't have any other choice.'

'No,' he agreed, 'you don't. Just as I have no other choice.'

He had gone before Karen could summon the strength for any further exchange. Not that there was a great deal left to say. She was going with him because she had nowhere else to go. To what exactly she had still to discover.

The leather suitcase that arrived a few moments later was accompanied by a leather handbag, neither of which she recognised. She rifled swiftly through the contents of the latter, finding a passport in her married name, along with a wallet containing a wad of foreign currency.

She had no idea of the worth. Nor did it make a great deal of difference to the present state of affairs. What she did wonder was just what plan she and this Lucio Fernandas had supposedly made.

There was nothing in the handbag to provide an answer to that question. She opened the suitcase, disconcerted by the jumble of clothing inside. Packed hastily and with little regard to content from the look of it, which suggested a decision made bare minutes before departure rather than a planned exit. Stuck in the middle of it all was a framed photograph that brought a lump to her throat. It had been taken on a camping holiday bare months before her parents had been killed. They were laughing together, holding up the tiny fish her mother had just caught in the river flowing behind them. A handsome pair, with everything to live for.

Julie would have sent it through along with the other things she'd asked for, Karen concluded, blinking the tears from her eyes. It would have been the last thing she'd have left behind, for certain.

She sorted out a pair of lace panties and matching bra, topping them with a white skirt and sleeveless cotton top she'd never to her knowledge seen before. There were only two pairs of shoes. She chose the pale beige sandals that were the only ones with a highish heel. At five feet six she was far from short, but she needed the boost to face a man over six feet in height with any degree of confidence at all.

The handbag yielded a pouch containing a pale pink lipstick, smoky eye-shadow and a mascara wand. No surprises there: she'd never used a lot of make-up. She donned the touch of lipstick she'd spoken of, and ran a comb through her dried hair. The bruising looked worse than it had the night before, as did the grazes on her cheek and jaw, but she had more to think about than her appearance.

Her last clear memories were of attending a leaving party for a workmate, followed by dinner out with a group from the office. Julie had been out herself when she had got back to the flat. She'd made a hot drink and gone straight to bed.

That had been the twelfth of September. The day before yesterday, so far as her mind was concerned. Luiz had said they'd been married three months, but that didn't tell her the date now.

He supplied an answer to that question on his return.

'It's the twenty-seventh of January,' he said. 'More

than halfway through our summer. The temperatures on the plateau are milder than here on the coast. While the days are hot at this time of the year, the humidity is low, the nights refreshingly cool.'

'It sounds good.' Karen was doing her utmost to stay on top of her emotions.

Luiz came to close and lock the suitcase she'd left open on the bed, hoisting it effortlessly up. 'I have a taxi waiting to take us to the hotel.'

'Hotel?' she queried.

'I think it better that the two of us spend some time together before returning to Guavada,' he said. 'We have a great deal to discuss.'

Karen forced herself into movement, reluctant to abandon the only bit of security she knew right now. Luiz went ahead to open the door for her, falling into step at her side to traverse a short, beautifully tiled corridor to a bank of lifts.

The one that arrived silently and smoothly in answer to his summons was empty. They descended without speaking, to emerge in a luxuriously appointed lobby. The receptionist on duty at a central desk bade them a smiling farewell, expressing what Karen took to be good wishes for the future. A forlorn hope indeed while the past months remained a blank.

Although it was still only a little after nine-thirty, the temperature outside was already soaring. Karen was glad to dive into the air-conditioned taxi-cab. With the suitcase stowed, Luiz slid in beside her. His thigh lay next to hers, the firm muscularity clearly defined beneath the fine cotton of his jeans when he moved.

Stripped, he would be magnificent, came the unbidden thought, bringing a sudden contraction deep down in the pit of her stomach. She would have seen him like that for certain—as he had no doubt seen her. She wondered how she, so unpractised in full-blown love-making, had managed to satisfy a man who would certainly have been no virgin.

They drove down through a city humming with workaday energies to a luxury hotel overlooking a superb crescent of white beach that was already heavily populated. Sugar Loaf reared now to the left, outlined against a sky beginning to cloud over a little.

'Is it going to rain, do you think?' Karen asked, turning from the balconied window—more for something to say than through any real interest in the weather. 'Summer is the rainy season out here, isn't it?'

Watching her from across the superbly furnished and decorated room, Luiz inclined his head. 'It is, yes.' His regard was penetrating. 'You recall that much then?'

'Not the way you mean,' she said. 'I must have read it somewhere.'

'Then the view out there means nothing to you?'

Karen's brows drew together. 'I've seen it in pictures.'

'But no more than that?'

'No.' Heart thudding against her ribcage, she added, 'What else might it mean?'

'It's the view you had from your room in this same hotel three months ago,' he said. 'Not the same room, I admit, but a replica of it. I hoped it might strike some spark of recollection.'

'It hasn't.' Her tone was flat. 'I must have won quite a lot to afford to stay in a place like this.'

'Several thousand pounds, I believe. A one-time opportunity to see how the other half lived, was how you excused the extravagance. There would have been little left to take home with you, for certain.'

'Except that I found myself a husband who *could* afford to stay in places like this.' She made a gesture of self-disgust. 'Forget I said that, will you?'

The dark head inclined again. 'It's forgotten.'

Considering his expression a moment ago, Karen doubted it. If she wanted to alienate him any more than he already must be alienated, considering the reason he'd followed her to Rio, she was going the right way about it.

He was leaning against a chest of drawers on the far side of the queen-size twin beds. Karen could only be thankful that there were two of them—although the thought of sharing even a room with him was daunting.

'I have the room next door,' he said, reading her mind with an ease she found daunting in itself. 'I've no intention of pressuring you into anything you find distasteful.'

'I'm sorry.' Karen scarcely knew what else to say. 'It isn't that I find you…unattractive.'

'A start, at least.' His tone was dry. 'Patience is no particular virtue of mine, but it seems I must learn to employ it. Perhaps sight of our home will help.'

'Perhaps.' Karen hesitated, reluctant to put the idea in his mind if it wasn't there already, yet needing reassurance. 'You don't think I'm pretending to have lost my memory, do you?'

His expression underwent an indefinable alteration. 'What might cause you to do such a thing?'

She lifted her shoulders. 'Fear of retribution, perhaps.'

'You see me as a wife-beater?'

'I don't know what you're capable of.' She was beginning to wish she'd kept her mouth shut. 'It isn't true, anyway. If I were capable of putting on that kind of act, I'd belong on the stage!'

'I believe you would.' His shoulders lifted. 'There have been moments in our relationship when you've sorely tried me, I admit.'

Karen eyed him in silence for a moment. 'We had rows?'

'We had some differences of opinion. You're a strong-willed young woman.'

'Where I come from, *all* women have minds of their own,' she claimed.

'As do Brazilian women—except that they are rather more subtle in their employment of it.' The pause was brief, the sudden change of tone emphatic. 'We have to put this behind us, and begin again.' He held up a staying hand as Karen started to speak. 'I'll arrange a hire car and show you the sights—the way I did when we first met. Perhaps then things will start to come back to you.'

He straightened away from the chest, turning towards the door. 'Come to the lobby in half an hour.'

Karen stood where she was for several moments after he'd left the room, mulling over everything that had been said. There were still so many questions to be answered, and only Luiz to supply those answers.

But was what he told her the whole truth? Why had she felt the need to turn to another man at all?

CHAPTER TWO

THE limousine Luiz had hired was already waiting for them outside when she went down. He put her into the front passenger seat before going round to slide behind the wheel.

He had shown her the sights this way when they'd first met, he'd said upstairs. If the hotel itself, plus the view from the window, had failed to stir her memory, it was unlikely that this was going to work either, but it was worth a try, Karen supposed. Anything was worth trying!

They headed for the mountains backing the city, leaving the congested streets to enter a world of tropical rainforest where thick lianas hung like pythons from tree branches furry with moss. The tangled canopy far above filtered out the sunlight, casting an eerie green glow over writhing creepers and huge tree ferns. There were flowers in abundance, their colours jewel-like among the foliage.

Karen was mesmerised, hardly able to believe that they were still within the city limits.

'It's like another planet!' she exclaimed, viewing a begonia bush bursting with bright yellow blossom and smothered in bees. 'What's making all the noise?'

'Monkeys,' Luiz advised. 'We invade their territory. This is the Terra da Tijuca, Rio's national park. It spreads over a hundred or more square miles.'

'It's wonderful!'

He cast a swift sideways glance at her rapt face. 'But in no way familiar?'

'No.' The enthusiasm faded as reality reared its head again. 'To the best of my knowledge, I've never seen any of this before.'

She sank back into her seat, head against the rest, eyes closed. 'I feel I'm living someone else's life!'

'I can assure you you're not,' Luiz responded. 'Your memory will return when you're ready to remember.'

Karen stole a glance at the hard-edged profile, feeling the fast-becoming-familiar tension in her lower body. 'Supposing that's never?'

His jaw compressed momentarily. 'Then we accept matters the way they are and live our lives accordingly.'

'I'm not sure I *can* accept it,' she said, and saw the compression come again.

'There's no other way.'

It was obvious that any further protest on her part would be a waste of time and breath, Karen acknowledged silently. Whatever she'd done, she was his wife and she was staying his wife.

Topped by the towering white statue of Christ, the granite peak of Corcovado afforded a panoramic view over both city and coastline. The skyscrapers below were reduced in size to toytown dimensions, the beaches of Copacabana and Impanema to curving crescents of white dotted with ants. Karen was overwhelmed by the sheer spectacle.

'You were equally impressed the first time you saw it,' said Luiz, watching her face as she gazed at the scene. 'As you were with everything.'

'Including yourself,' she murmured.

'Including myself,' he agreed. 'As I intended you to be.'

'How long did I hold out?'

Dark brows lifted. 'Hold out?'

'Before you got me into bed with you?'

It was a moment before he answered, his tone quizzical. 'Does it matter to you?'

'Yes,' she said. 'I need to know.'

His shrug was brief. 'We made love on the first night of our acquaintance.'

Karen swallowed. 'You must have thought me the easiest conquest you'd ever made!'

'No such thought entered my mind,' he denied. 'We were two people drawn by the same overwhelming force.'

She couldn't bring herself to meet the dark eyes full on. 'Would you still have wanted to marry me if I'd had previous experience?'

'I would have accepted it, yes.'

Karen looked at him then, oblivious to the other people on the platform. An arm resting against the guard rail, head outlined against the sky, he looked at ease in a way she envied. She had a sudden urge to disrupt that equanimity.

'Tell me about Lucio Fernandas,' she said with deliberation. 'Who exactly is he?'

She gained her wish as his face hardened. 'I prefer not to speak of him.'

'We *have* to talk about him,' she insisted.

Straightened now away from the rail, Luiz studied her for a moment in silence. When he spoke it was in tautly controlled tones. 'There's little enough I can tell you of his background. He was employed by one of my foremen. Had I had any notion...' He broke off, gritting his teeth together. 'Suffice to say he would have been in no fit state to arouse *any* woman's interest!'

Karen's chest felt tight as a drum. Luiz Andrade was a proud man; it didn't take intimate knowledge to be aware of that. The discovery that his wife had been having an affair at all would have hit him hard enough, but for her to have become involved with a mere employee!

'I'm still not convinced it's the truth,' she said defensively. 'What actual proof do you have that there was any affair to start with?'

Amber lights glinted in the depths of his eyes. 'What proof do I need other than that you provided yourself in running off with him?'

'There had to be some prior signs, surely?'

'There apparently were, had I been willing to see them. Beatriz suspected, but failed to warn me.'

Karen put up an involuntary hand to her temple as pain lanced briefly through it. There was an odd buzzing in her ears, a sense of being drawn somewhere she didn't want to go.

Luiz moved swiftly to catch her as she swayed, arms sliding about her to hold her close. She could feel the strong beat of his heart at her breast, the sun-stoked heat of his body.

'I'm all right now,' she managed. 'Just a bit of a dizzy spell, that's all.'

He made no attempt to stop her as she pulled away from him. 'I should have refused to discuss the matter,' he said. 'This isn't the place.'

What attention they'd drawn from those in the vicinity had now been returned to the scenery. Karen tilted her head to let the breeze cool her cheeks, both hands on the guardrail to steady herself.

'Who is Beatriz?'

Luiz made a curt gesture. 'As I said, this isn't the place. We'll return to the hotel.'

She made no protest. The name had meant something to her, that was obvious, but there was no further break in the curtain.

It was well into the afternoon when they reached the hotel again. Luiz accepted Karen's plea that she was tired and needed rest rather than food without demur, simply saying that he would see her later.

A shower was a first priority on reaching her room. She luxuriated for several minutes in the glass-walled cabinet, blanking out everything but the feel of the water streaming over her skin.

Towelled dry, she donned the robe provided and returned to the bedroom to extract fresh underwear from the suitcase. There seemed little point in unpacking fully when she had no idea how long they would be here.

Her throat closed up at the thought of what she would be facing when they did return to the ranch. However much she might want to disbelieve it, all the evidence pointed to the fact that she really had been having an affair with another man.

Where would she have been now, she wondered, if there had been no accident? What kind of life would she have had with a man capable of leaving her lying unconscious in the road? How could she have been drawn to another man at all when she was married to one as charismatic as Luiz Andrade?

Unless Luiz wasn't the man *he* appeared to be either. How could she be sure what their marital relationship had really been like? There had been rows, that much he'd admitted. She only had his word that there had been no serious rift between them.

He left her alone until eight, by which time she had begun to wonder if he had deserted her after all. When he did put in an appearance he was wearing a light linen suit that sat on his frame as if made to measure.

'I felt the need of fresh clothing,' he said. 'You at least have that facility.' He ran an appraising glance over her slender curves in the lilac silk tunic that had been one of the few items in the suitcase she considered suitable for dining out. 'Did you rest well?'

Karen turned away, unable to hold his gaze for long. 'As well as can be expected, considering. What happens now?'

'We have dinner here in the hotel. If we repeat, as far as is possible, the details of our time here together, perhaps it will stir something in your memory.'

'*Every* detail?' she asked after a moment.

'I said as far as is possible,' he responded. 'I make no demands on you.'

'For now,' she murmured, and heard him draw a roughened breath.

'Do you think me so easily able to banish the thought of you with Fernandas from my head? Whenever I close my eyes I see you in his arms!'

Karen made herself look at him, seeing the anger glittering his eyes. 'I'm sorry,' she said wretchedly. 'I wasn't thinking.' She paused, searching for words. 'Do you think you ever will be able to put it aside?'

'If not I must learn to live with it.' He was in control again, though his voice remained taut. 'The marriage will not be dissolved.'

There was nothing she could say to that. Nothing

likely to help the situation. But there were still so many things she needed to know.

'This morning you mentioned someone called Beatriz,' she ventured. 'Who is she?'

Something flickered deep in the dark eyes. 'She's the wife of my brother, Raymundo.'

The latter name struck no chord either. 'Does he work on the ranch too?'

'He and Beatriz have their home there,' came the somewhat ambiguous reply. 'As does my young sister too. Regina was devastated by your leaving.'

Karen sank to a seat, her legs no longer supportive. Just how many people *would* she be facing on her return to the home she had fled?

'How old is Regina?' she asked.

'Eighteen now.'

Green eyes lifted to view the incisive features. 'And Raymundo?'

'Twenty-eight. Four years younger than myself. There was another brother between us in age, but he died some two years ago.'

Empathy came swiftly, born of her own loss. 'I'm sorry.'

'You never knew him.' Luiz moved abruptly, crossing to open a cabinet Karen hadn't attempted to explore. 'I think we're both in need of a stimulant.'

He poured a colourless liquid for them both, bringing both glasses back to where she sat to thrust one into her hand. Not gin, she realised, putting it to her lips, but white rum. The spirit burned her throat, but she finished it, glad of the immediate effect. Alcohol was no solution to her problems, for certain, but it helped take the edge off them.

'What about parents?' she said.

'I lost my father some years ago. My mother married again, and now lives in Brasilia.'

Karen viewed the empty glass in her hand with lacklustre eyes. 'Have we met?'

'Just the once, when I took you to visit her.'

'Did she approve? Of the marriage, I mean?'

'No.' His tone was unemotional. 'She would have preferred that I marry a woman of my own race.'

'That's understandable.'

'It's of no consequence.' His own glass also drained, he took hers from her unresisting hand, depositing both on the nearest surface. 'Enough questions for now. You need to eat.'

Food was the farthest thing from her mind, but she rose obediently to her feet. It would be embarrassing going into a restaurant looking like this, she acknowledged, catching sight of her face in a nearby wall mirror, but there was little to be done about it.

There were others in the lift descending to the ground floor. Karen could feel the glances. If Luiz was aware of them too, he gave no sign. The subdued lighting in the restaurant afforded some comfort. All the same, it was a relief to gain the relative privacy of the alcove table.

There was nothing in the least bit familiar about the plush surroundings. She hadn't really expected there to be. She left it to Luiz to choose her meal, eating what was put in front of her without tasting a thing. The wine he'd ordered went straight to her head. She drank only half a glass, afraid of losing her grip altogether.

'This isn't going to work,' she said bleakly over coffee. She cast a glance at the man seated opposite, senses stirred by his dark masculinity. 'I don't think anything is.'

'There's nothing to be lost by trying,' he said. 'From here we went to a club.' His gaze was on her face. 'And then back to the hotel.'

Karen felt a pulse throb suddenly at her temple, setting her heart pounding in empathy. She tried desperately to grasp the image that fleeted through her mind.

'What is it?' Luiz's voice was low but urgent. 'Do you remember?'

She slowly shook her head. 'Just a feeling for a moment. Nothing concrete.'

'But it meant *something* to you, that was apparent.'

'It seems so.' She studied the vital features, wishing she could tell what he was thinking right now. 'Does everyone know about Lucio Fernandas?'

The glitter sprang in his eyes for a moment, then subsided again. 'Beatriz is the only one with that information.'

'You trust her to keep it to herself?'

'She had better do so. Regina believes you left merely because of dissidence between us. Your amnesia will be difficult enough for her to accept.'

Not nearly as difficult as it was for her, Karen thought. Recollection might not be palatable, but it had to be better than this blankness.

'We could always try keeping it a secret,' she said, and saw his lips thin.

'You find the situation one to treat with flippancy?'

She made a small apologetic gesture. 'No, of course not. It's just...' She paused, swallowing thickly. 'Have you any idea what it's like to sit here and listen to you telling me about people and places and matters I've absolutely no concept of? The person I seem to have become bears no relationship to the person I believe myself to be. It's like looking in a mirror and seeing someone else's reflection!'

Luiz inclined his head, face set. 'Difficult for both of us. To be deceived is bad, but to be forgotten...'

He left it there, lifting a hand to signal to the waiter. Up to now, Karen had been too involved with her own feelings to give any real thought to what he must be going through. She tried to put herself in his shoes, to imagine how it must feel to be wiped completely from her mind after months of living together as husband and wife. What man could handle that with equanimity?

She watched him sign the bill that was brought to the table. Those lean, long-fingered hands would know every inch of her, came the thought, sending a *frisson* the length of her spine. In three months she would no doubt have got over any inhibitions she might have had herself: the way her body was reacting at this moment gave every indication of it. She might not remember loving this man, but she was vitally attracted by him. Whatever had driven her to seek another man's arms, it couldn't have been because Luiz no longer stirred her.

She made an effort to compose herself as the waiter departed, to meet the eyes raised to her. 'What now?' she asked.

'As I said before, we follow the same pattern.'

'You really think it's going to help?'

'Whatever chance there is of stirring something in your memory, we must take,' he stated. He got to his feet, rounding the table to draw out her chair. 'The night is still young.'

It was gone ten o'clock, Karen saw from the thin

gold watch on his wrist as she rose. Handsome, charismatic, obviously not without money, it could be said that Luiz Andrade was everything any woman could possibly want. Yet she had left him for a man whose backbone, it seemed, was so weak he had left her lying in the road. It didn't make sense.

They took a taxi to what appeared at first sight to be a large private residence. Luiz handed over a card in the well-appointed entrance hall, and they were duly signed in to wander at will through rooms devoted to various pastimes.

Luiz ignored the crowded casino, leading the way to a smaller, dimly lit room where couples swayed to the beat of an excellent four-piece combo. There were tables set around the periphery of the room, but he ignored those too, drawing her on to the floor and into his arms.

Held against the hard male body, Karen concentrated on matching her steps to his. She felt his hand warm at her centre back, his breath stirring the hair at her temple. Her mouth was in line with the hollow of his throat, revealed by the open neckline of his shirt; the male scent of him tantalised her nostrils.

All sensations of the present not the past, she told herself. Luiz was a man to whom any woman with an ounce of red blood in her veins would respond. Perhaps if they actually made love…

She rejected the thought immediately. Even if she could bring herself to try such an experiment, Luiz almost certainly wouldn't with the images he'd spoken of earlier crowding his mind. He had followed her to Rio with the intention of fetching her back because his pride wouldn't allow him any other course, but that wasn't to say he'd have been prepared to make love to her again.

'Could it have worked even if I hadn't lost my memory?' she heard herself ask. 'Forcing me back, I mean.'

It was a moment or two before Luiz answered. When he did speak his tone was unemotional. 'I would have found it difficult to put your transgressions aside, I admit. Trust isn't easily restored.'

'But you still wouldn't have been prepared to finish it?'

'No. Marriage, in my eyes, is for life. The reason why I waited so long to find the woman I could live that life with.'

'Only she let you down,' Karen said huskily. 'I can't tell you how awful it makes me feel to think I'm capable of that kind of behaviour! I still find it hard to believe I *could* be capable of it.'

'There was no mistake,' he said. 'Only the one you made in choosing a man who cared so little for you that he left you sprawled in the dust.'

Karen rode the hurt as best as she was able. 'What's even harder to explain is why a man like that would have abandoned a good job.'

Luiz gave a short laugh. 'Fear of what would happen to him when I discovered the affair would have been incentive enough.'

'In which case,' she pursued, 'why would he have taken the risk in the first place?'

The laugh came again. 'You do yourself an injustice. Few men could remain indifferent to you. You were a virgin when we met only because you'd never known one capable of bringing the fires smouldering within you to life. I could have taken you within minutes of our meeting.'

'So why didn't you?' she challenged.

'Because I wanted more than just your body.' His voice had softened in reminiscence. 'I wanted every part of you.'

All thought suspended, Karen felt heat rising through her from a central core, a spreading weakness in her limbs. Her body moved instinctively against him, pressing closer to his hardness.

'Stop that!' he said harshly.

She came back to earth with a jolt as reality raised its ugly head again, her face flaming as she looked up into the sparking dark eyes.

'It wasn't intentional,' she stammered. 'It just…happened.'

His lip curled. 'The way it just happened with Fernandas?'

'How can I know?' she asked wretchedly. 'How can I know anything for certain? All I have to go on is what you tell me.'

Luiz stopped moving, the spark grown to a blaze. 'Are you accusing me of lying to you?'

'No, of course not. But unless this Lucio Fernandas had money of his own, none of it adds up. The money I had on me almost certainly wouldn't have been enough to take the two of us very far.'

'So why else would the two of you have been on the same flight? Why else, for that matter, would you have been on the flight at all?'

Karen shook her head, feeling ever more desperate. 'I can't answer that. All I do know is…'

'Is?' he prompted as she broke off.

What she'd been about to say was that she simply

couldn't visualise walking out on someone who could make her feel the way he'd made her feel just now, but she wasn't ready to go down that particular road.

'Nothing,' she said. 'Can we call it a day? I have a dreadful headache.'

Anger gave way to concern. 'The fault is mine for insisting on continuing the attempt. I'll arrange for a taxi to be called.'

He was solicitousness itself while they waited for the taxi to arrive. Karen hadn't lied about the headache; it felt as if a hammer was beating at the space between her eyes. And this was just the beginning. There was worse to come. Facing the rest of the family would tax her resources to the limit.

It was coming up to midnight when they reached the hotel. Luiz had the receptionist on duty procure some painkillers and a glass of water for her before taking the lift to their floor.

'I trust the headache will soon subside,' he said at her door. For a moment he seemed to hesitate, his eyes on her pale face, then he said a brief goodnight and moved on to the room next door.

Thankful to be alone at last, Karen shed her clothing and took a shower. The bathroom was lined in mirror glass. She studied herself clinically as she towelled dry. Breasts high, waist slim, hips smoothly rounded, her body was, she knew from past experience, a magnet for male eyes, her face, in normal times, an equal draw. She'd had several short-term romances, but had lost hope of ever meeting any man who could make her want him the way he wanted her.

Until coming here to Rio and meeting Luiz Andrade. The very thought of him sent a ripple down her spine. The mistake she'd probably made then was in confusing lust with love. A mistake she must have realised eventually.

Regardless, she just couldn't imagine herself turning to another man for solace. Especially one like this Lucio Fernandas. Could she possibly have been so desperate that she'd cultivate a relationship with him simply to secure his help in getting away from Guavada?

She was going round in circles again, she acknowledged wearily, and still getting nowhere. The only chance she had of learning the truth was by returning to Guavada. Not that she had any choice in the matter anyway.

Worn out, she slept like a log, awakening to sunlight and a low-pitched ringing that turned out to be the telephone on the bedside cabinet.

'How are you feeling?' Luiz asked.

'Better,' she said, referring to the headache not the inner turbulence. 'What time is it?'

'Gone ten o'clock. You missed breakfast, but I can have something brought to the room.'

She wasn't hungry, Karen started to say, breaking off as her stomach growled a protest. 'Give me ten minutes,' she said instead.

'What would you like?'

'Fruit and coffee will be fine.'

She put the receiver down, wondering how she could speak so calmly and collectedly when her insides were dancing a fandango at the mere sound of his voice. They'd made love the night before her departure, he'd said yesterday. If it was the truth, whatever had gone wrong between them hadn't affected her physical responses even at that point.

Showered, she donned the white robe and went to open up the balcony doors with the intention of eating outside. She closed them again hastily on feeling the sticky heat, glad of the cool blast from the air-conditioning vents. São Paulo was far less humid than this, Luiz had said; she could be glad of that at least.

A knock at the door heralded the arrival of a waiter with a table trolley containing far more than the items she had requested. Luiz followed the man in, despatching him with what appeared to be a whole handful of banknotes. It was unlikely to be payment on the spot in a place like this, Karen concluded, so it had to be a tip. Generous or not, she had no way of knowing.

He was wearing the suit from last night, this time with a black shirt. Opened a little lower at the neckline than the night before, it revealed a fine gold chain bearing a small medal, the latter nestling amidst a curly mat of hair.

'I only asked for fruit and coffee,' she said, pulse rate increasing by the minute. She indicated the cereal, the covered tureen containing who knew what, the rolls and preserves. 'I can't eat all that!'

From the look in the dark eyes, her instinctive move to tighten the tie belt of the robe had not gone unnoted, though he made no comment. 'It's of no consequence,' he declared. 'The choice is there should you change your mind. I'll take coffee with you.'

Feeling distinctly vulnerable, she poured for them both, leaving his black as he'd requested the previous night. Luiz accepted the cup from her to set it down on the small table at the side of a nearby chair.

'I reserved seats on the one-thirty shuttle to São Paulo,' he announced without preamble. 'You were right last night. Attempting to recreate our beginnings is a waste of time and effort. All we can do is return to Guavada and hope for an eventual cure.'

Karen took a couple of deep swallows from her own cup before answering, needing the stimulant. 'What do we tell your sister?'

'She already knows about the amnesia. I spoke to her earlier. She sends her love, and hopes to help in your recovery.'

'And the others?'

'Regina is to pass on the news. If you're concerned for what Beatriz might say, you can rest assured of her silence,' he added hardily.

'You think she won't even have told your brother the real reason I went?'

He hesitated. 'Perhaps that would be asking a little too much. There should be no secrets between husband and wife.'

Karen busied herself slicing a banana into a dish, adding grapes and ready-cut pieces of melon. 'As manager of the ranch, I suppose you hold a lot of authority,' she murmured.

'I don't manage the ranch,' he said. 'I own it.'

Her head came up. 'You *own* it?'

'Why such surprise?' he asked on an ironical note. 'Do I appear a man of small means?'

'No,' she acknowledged. 'Not at all. I just thought…' She broke off, lifting her shoulders. 'I'm not sure what I thought. Is your brother a partner?'

'No.' The statement was unequivocal. 'Are you going to eat the fruit, or simply continue poking at it?'

Karen forked up a piece of banana and put it in her mouth, chewing on it resolutely. Fruit here had a far better taste than back home, she had to admit. Except that England was home no longer, of course. Not for her. She might never even see it again!

'Is it far to the airport?' she asked, shutting out the hovering despondency.

'The São Paulo shuttle flies from Aeroporto Santos Dumont in the city centre,' Luiz returned. The flight itself takes less than an hour, the drive to Guavada considerably longer, but we should be there before dark.'

To meet more people she couldn't remember. People who had known *her* a whole three months. How, Karen wondered numbly, was she to deal with it all?

CHAPTER THREE

THE flight was short and uneventful. Luiz had left a Land Rover at the São Paulo airport on his way out, prompting Karen to wonder how she and this Lucio had got there themselves. If in a car, it must still be parked here somewhere.

She didn't care to broach the subject. Any mention of Lucio Fernandas was like waving a red rag before a bull.

By four o'clock they had left the city suburbs well behind and were driving through a landscape of grassy, tree-dotted plains broken by isolated low ranges. As Luiz had promised, the climate up here, some two thousand feet above sea level, was far pleasanter than Rio's.

Karen recognised nothing. Not that she'd expected to. The closer they came to the home she had abandoned just a few days ago, the worse she felt. Beatriz may be the only one to know the real reason she had flown, but the others were hardly going to see a supposed disagreement with Luiz as an adequate reason. There was every chance that her partial amnesia would be suspect to them, if not to Luiz himself. It was, she had to acknowledge, a very convenient method of avoiding responsibility for her actions.

'Are you feeling unwell?' Luiz asked, shooting her a glance. 'Do you wish to stop?'

Karen shook her head, pulling herself together. 'Just nervousness. How are they likely to react?'

He gave a faint smile. 'If I know my sister, she will throw her arms about you and commiserate. She blames me for driving you away with my domineering manner.'

'Are you?' Karen ventured. 'Domineering, I mean?'

'No more than I have to be to maintain your respect. We come from different cultures. There were adjustments to be made by each of us. I believed we had achieved a balance.'

'When I ruined everything by going off with another man,' Karen said hollowly. 'I still can't imagine how I could have done that. To leave…'

'To leave?' Luiz prompted as she let the words trail away.

Like the night before, she'd been about to say, To leave a man like you, but it still sounded too much like sycophancy. 'Without even a word,' she substituted. 'The whole thing was shameful!'

It was a moment before Luiz responded, his expression austere again. 'We must put it behind us.'

'*Can* you, though?' she asked.

'As I've said before, I have no choice.'

There was little comfort in the answer. Karen hadn't really expected any. It was still difficult to accept that the person she had been—the person she still felt herself to be inside—could have behaved in the manner ascribed to her. As if someone else had taken over her body during the lost months.

'Tell me about the ranch,' she said after a moment or two, desperate for something to break the silence between them.

Eyes on the road, Luiz lifted his shoulders in a brief shrug. 'What can I tell you? Guavada produces beef for the export markets. It was founded in my grandfather's day, the land area increased over the years to become what it is today.'

'You own a third share then?'

'As the eldest son, I inherited outright ownership.' His lips slanted when she failed to comment. 'I sense disapproval.'

Karen stole a swift glance at the hard-cut profile. 'It seems a bit unfair, that's all. In England all the children would be entitled to a share—male *and* female.'

'This is not England,' came the short response. 'Raymundo is no pauper. He could found businesses of his own. As to Regina, she bears the name only until she marries.'

'Is that imminent?'

'Regina has yet to meet someone capable of retaining her interest for longer than a few weeks.'

'Well, at eighteen she has plenty of time. After all...'

'After all, *I* waited long enough to find the right person,' he finished for her on a sardonic note as she broke off.

'What you obviously believed was the right person at the time,' she said, gathering her resources once more. 'We can all make mistakes.'

'Especially when judgement is clouded by a lovely face and body.'

'I doubt that you'd have allowed your libido to rule you to such an extent.' Karen kept her tone level with an effort. 'Any more than I would myself.'

Luiz made no reply. He looked remote again. Karen leaned back against the seat rest and closed her eyes, willing herself to stay in control. Whatever happened from here-on-in, she could only go along with it.

They drove through a sizeable township bright with

greenery, turning off the road on to a narrower one some fifteen minutes later, to pass beneath a tall wooden archway with the name carved into its surface.

Fencing stretched to either hand as far as the eye could see, though with no sign of either cattle or habitation. The latter proved to be hidden behind a large clump of trees a half mile or so ahead.

Anticipating something akin to the ranch houses seen in cowboy films, Karen was totally thrown by the lovely colonial-style building that came into view. Fronted by beautifully landscaped lawns, its white walls glinting in the late afternoon sunlight, it had verandas running the whole way round.

The girl who came out from the house as the car drew to a standstill was an Andrade through and through, her waist-length hair darkly luxuriant about her vibrant young face, her figure, clad casually in shorts and sleeveless top, lithe and lovely. As Luiz had predicted, she gave no quarter to the amnesia, descending the steps with open arms and a radiant smile.

'So wonderful to have you home with us again!' she declared. 'But your poor face! How it must pain you!'

'Not any more,' Karen assured her. 'And the marks will soon be gone too.' She found a smile of her own, overcoming the awkwardness of the moment by sheer willpower. 'Perhaps my memory will have returned by then.'

The shadow that passed across her sister-in-law's face was come and gone in an instant. 'It will! I'm sure of it!'

'I think refreshment would be a priority at present,' said Luiz with a questioning look at Karen. 'A cold drink, perhaps?'

She hesitated. 'I don't suppose tea would be available?'

'Of course.' His tone was tinged with humour for a moment. 'You insisted on it. Too much coffee, you said, was bad for the health.'

Mood lifting a little, she tried a lighter tone herself. 'Not very tactful in a coffee-producing country!'

'I like tea too,' claimed Regina. 'I'll have some prepared immediately.' She held out an inviting hand. 'Come.'

Karen accompanied her indoors to a wide hall. A wrought-iron staircase rose from the centre to branch off left and right to open galleries. Plant-life abounded, spilling from standing pots, from hanging baskets, from the galleries themselves.

The woman who appeared in an archway under the curve of the staircase was in her mid-twenties. Unlike Regina's, her hair was a dark blonde; her striking features were formed from a totally different mould, her figure voluptuous. There was no welcome in the tawny eyes, just a cold watchfulness.

She spoke in Portuguese, drawing a sharp admonishment from Luiz.

'We will all of us speak only English when Karen is present. The way we did when she first came to Guavada.'

'Does that mean I learned to speak Portuguese myself?' Karen asked, picking up on the nuances.

'You acquired a fair grasp,' he confirmed.

She found that difficult to take in. She'd shown little aptitude for compulsory French in school, much less other languages.

On the other hand, she'd never lived in a foreign speaking household before.

'You expect us all to believe this claim of yours?' demanded the newcomer, who could only be Beatriz.

'What you believe is your affair,' Luiz cut in hardily before Karen could form an answer. 'What you *say* in this house is mine. Where is Raymundo?'

'He had to go out.' Beatriz both looked and sounded resentful of the warning, but obviously wasn't prepared to make an issue of it. 'Some problem.'

'Then we'll see him at dinner. Have the tea sent up,' he added to his sister.

He took Karen's arm to guide her up the iron-balustraded staircase, creating havoc with her hard-won equilibrium. She was torn between two opposing fires when he released her at the top of the stairs, a part of her relieved to be free of his touch, another, deeper, part yearning for even closer contact.

The room to which he led the way lay towards the end of the open gallery. It was large and airy, the carved dark wood furnishings relieved by white walls and lush fabrics. The panelled windows were shuttered in slatted wood.

The wide bed drew Karen's eyes. It would, she reckoned, sleep four with ease. She had shared that bed with the man at her side—made love with him in the dark of night. The thought alone made her quiver.

'Your bathroom lies through there,' said Luiz, indicating a door in the far wall. 'The other door gives access to my room.' He registered her expression with an ironic slant of his lips. 'A matter of tradition still sometimes upheld in our culture—although we made little use of it.'

He was standing close. Karen had a sudden mad urge to turn and put her arms about his neck, her lips to his; to seek a way back to what she had lost. Only the fear of rejection kept her from giving way. It would take time, he'd admitted, to put the images of her in another man's arms aside. She could hardly blame him for that.

Her suitcase was brought by a young man dressed in dark trousers and white shirt, whom Karen could only assume was a servant. He gave her a curious glance, but said nothing, depositing the suitcase on a stand at the foot of the bed and departing. No doubt, she reflected wryly, to speculate with others on the return of the errant wife.

Luiz had moved to a window, standing with hands thrust into trouser pockets, gazing out on to landscaped grounds lush with foliage.

'We must find a way,' he said. 'There can be no going back, only forward.'

'I know.' Karen's voice was husky, her throat tight. 'It isn't going to be easy for either of us.'

He swung to look at her, lips twisting as he took in the pallor of her face, the shadows beneath her eyes. 'You dread the thought of renewing our relationship?'

'I dread the thought of living with this blankness for the rest of my life,' she prevaricated.

'It may not come to that. The doctor told me you could recover your memory at any moment.'

He would also have told him that the longer the amnesia went on the less likely it was to end, Karen suspected. She gazed at him in silence, willing him to take the first step towards the renewal he had spoken of. He still wanted her; she could sense that much in him. It could be a way back. It might be the *only* way back.

The arrival of the tea, borne this time by a young woman, put paid to any move he might have made.

'I'll leave you to refresh yourself in peace,' he said. 'Dinner is at nine. I'd suggest you take advantage of the time to rest. You look exhausted.'

She felt it. Both emotionally and physically. Lonely too, when he'd gone. She had been mistress of this household for a whole three months. A role she would be expected to take on again if the marriage was to continue in any sense at all. The very idea was daunting.

Drained though she was, sleep was farthest from her mind at present. She drank the tea gratefully, then took a look in the bathroom, finding it equipped with every luxury.

The cabinet above the ornate vanity unit held an array of expensive feminine toiletries, the brand name the same as the ones she had found in her suitcase back at the hospital. She closed the door again, faced by her reflection in the mirror fronting it. The grazes were already beginning to heal, the bruise at her temple to lighten a little in hue. In another few days—a week at the most—there would be no outward sign of the accident left, her looks fully restored. For what that was worth.

Back in the bedroom, she tentatively tried the connecting door, finding it locked. According to Luiz, he'd spent little time in there, but he would almost certainly be doing it tonight. For how many other nights remained to be seen. Whatever else had been lost, the physical attraction between them was still strong. It was all she had to cling to.

A walk-in closet held a variety of garments. She fingered through them, looking for something—*anything*—recognisable. There was nothing. She could only think she must have acquired a whole new wardrobe for her trip to Rio.

The surface of the highly polished dark wood dressing table was bare. Tucked away in a drawer, she at last found some familiar items: the silver-backed hair brushes her parents had given her on her eighteenth birthday; two ballet dancer figurines; the antique silver box she used to hold tissues. None of them worth a great deal in monetary terms, but sentimentally irreplaceable.

There must be other things somewhere—these, and the photograph of her parents, couldn't be all she had asked Julie to send—but they sufficed to give her some feeling of home.

Someone must have been in here and cleared them away, she reflected. Hardly the kind of thing the servants would take it on themselves to do, and she doubted if either Regina or Raymundo was the culprit. Which left only Beatriz.

The woman's animus had been only too apparent. Considering what she knew, it was hardly unexpected. Hardly so surprising either that she might suspect her of fabricating the amnesia in order to protect herself from Luiz's anger.

Weariness finally overcame her. With almost three hours to go until dinner, there was plenty of time to take the sleep Luiz had advised. She was going to need all the stamina she could muster to get through the evening.

The room was lamplit when she opened her eyes, the shutters closed on the outside world. She hadn't undressed before lying down on the bed, but someone had still seen fit to cover her with a light throw. Luiz? she wondered.

It was just gone eight, she saw from the clock on the bedside table. Her head felt heavy when she sat up, her eyes filled with grains of sand. She had to force herself to her feet.

A shower went some way towards refreshing her, although she'd left herself with no time to wash and dry her hair as she would have liked to do. She used a tortoiseshell clip she found in a drawer to pin it back into her nape.

Going by the style of clothing she had found, dress here was more casual than formal. She donned a swirly skirt in mingled colours, along with a white top scooped low at the neckline, viewing her image with a spark of interest. A very different look from her normal, or what had been normal, style, but she had to admit it suited her.

With no further excuse to linger, and with the time approaching the set hour, she nerved herself to leave the room. The man standing in the wide hall below looked up as she paused at the gallery rail, the expression that crossed his face at the sight of her too swiftly come and gone for analysis.

The resemblance between him and Luiz was too marked for him to be anyone other than the brother. Karen drew a steadying breath.

'You must be Raymundo.'

Dark head tipped back, he viewed her for a long moment in silence. 'So it's true,' he said at length. 'You have no memory of me.'

'Not of anyone,' she confirmed. 'I'm…sorry.'

'A dreadful thing to happen.' He sounded genuinely sympathetic. 'Are you coming down?'

Cheered a little by the lack of censure—assuming his wife had told him about Lucio Fernandas—she moved to the staircase and descended to join him. He was shorter than Luiz by an inch or two, she judged, though no less fit.

He said something in Portuguese, shaking his head as if in recollection. 'It's good to have you back,' he amended softly. 'Soon you'll be speaking our language again.'

'I can't imagine it right now, but I'll do my best,' she returned, sparking a sudden smile.

'We'll all of us do that.' He extended an arm. 'You will allow me to guide you?'

He meant to the dining room, of course. She had, Karen acknowledged, not the slightest idea which of the doors leading off the hall it might lay behind.

'Thanks,' she said gratefully.

They found the rest of the family already seated in a room which, though well appointed, was very much smaller than she would have anticipated in a house of this size and stature. The table itself was round, and would seat no more than six.

'This is where we eat as a family,' Raymundo explained, as if sensing her confusion. 'The dining room is only used for more formal entertaining.' His eyes were on his brother, who had risen from his place. 'Karen was lost. She needed to be shown the way.'

Face unrevealing, Luiz moved to pull out the chair at his side in mute invitation. Karen slid into it, feeling anything but comfortable, aware of Beatriz's eyes on her from across the table. She didn't need to look to know what they held. The enmity was searing.

Raymundo took his own seat between the two of them, with Regina closing the circle.

'You look so much less tired than when you arrived,' exclaimed the latter warmly. 'The rest has been good for you.'

'You slept deeply,' said Luiz. 'You failed to stir even when I closed the window shutters.'

'It's been a long day.' Karen made the comment as light as possible. It was going to seem an even longer night, she judged, but it had to be endured. It all had to be endured. Beatriz wasn't going to make life easy for her for certain.

Hungry by now, she ate her fill of the delicious seafood stew that constituted the main part of the meal. *Moqueca*, Regina told her it was called. She refused both the coffee that ended the ritual and the tea that was offered, finishing off her wine instead. She longed to retire to the privacy of her bedroom again, yet at the same time dreaded the thought of the lonely hours to come.

Luiz had said little at all during the meal. Karen could see his hand on the periphery of her vision as he lifted the coffee cup to his lips. Her husband: the man she had married with what appeared to be scarcely a moment's real thought about what she was doing. Even while she could appreciate how bowled over she would have been by him on sight alone, it had been an utterly mad impulse to follow. She hadn't known him any better then than she knew him now. Not in any proper sense.

Julie must have thought she was utterly crazy. *She* certainly would have if the positions had been reversed. Except that Julie would never have got herself into such a situation. Her feet were far too firmly on the ground.

If she'd stayed in touch with her it was possible that she'd told her what was going on. The only way to find out was to put Julie in the picture regarding her memory loss and ask, although she shrank from the thought.

'Your head hurts?' Luiz asked, bringing her to the sudden realisation that she had a hand to her temple.

'It aches a little,' she admitted truthfully.

'Then you must rest again.' He got to his feet, coming behind her to draw back her chair. 'Sleep is the best healer.'

For the body, perhaps, she thought. It made little difference to her mental state.

'I'll say goodnight then,' she proffered to the table at large, avoiding any direct contact with Beatriz's gaze.

'Tomorrow,' said Regina purposefully, 'we will renew your acquaintance with La Santa.'

'The town we passed through,' Luiz supplied.

'It's market day tomorrow,' Regina continued. 'You like the market.'

Karen could imagine. She always had liked them. She smiled at the girl. 'I'll look forward to it.'

Expecting to be left to find her own way back to her room, she was disconcerted when Luiz accompanied her.

'You don't need to do this,' she said in the outer hall. 'I'll be quite all right.'

'You look far from all right,' he returned shortly. 'I'm in need of rest myself, so you've nothing to fear from me tonight.'

'I don't fear you,' she denied. 'I just...' She spread her hands in a helpless little gesture. 'It's so hard to know *what* to say!'

'Then say nothing,' he advised. 'Only time will tell

whether our marriage can be made good again. But be assured, good or not, it will continue.'

There was nothing she *could* say to that, Karen acknowledged painfully.

CHAPTER FOUR

AWAKE at seven-thirty, Karen was downstairs by eight, to find Luiz and Raymundo had already breakfasted and gone about whatever business they had. What time they might return was apparently anyone's guess.

The meal was served out on the veranda at the rear of the house. Eating the fruit that was all she had appetite for, Karen felt pinioned beneath Beatriz's steely gaze. She was grateful for Regina's efforts to lighten the atmosphere.

The day was already warm, with a promise of higher temperatures to come. It would have been October when she had first arrived: a brand new bride, too head-over-heels in love with the man she'd known bare days to view her new world through anything but the most rose-tinted of glasses.

How long, she wondered, had it taken for reality to kick in? How long before she'd begun to regret abandoning everything and everyone she knew to settle in a country totally alien to her? Life here was so different from what she'd been accustomed to. Had she ever really adjusted to it?

'You mentioned reintroducing me to La Santa today,' she said to Regina, doing her best to ignore Beatriz's heavy presence. 'Do you still feel like it?'

'Of course.' The girl hesitated a moment. 'You realise word of your amnesia will already have spread.'

'It would be a difficult secret to keep,' Karen

agreed, trying to be practical about it. 'At least I shan't be expected to recognise people on sight.'

Silent up until now, Beatriz said something short and sharp beneath her breath, then rose abruptly to her feet to stalk indoors. Karen caught Regina's eye and gave a helpless little shrug.

'Pay no attention,' the younger girl advised. 'She was always jealous of you. You took the position she would have occupied herself had Luiz been willing. Raymundo is my brother too, and I love him dearly, but he can never be more than second best in Beatriz's eyes.'

Taken aback, Karen sought a response. 'That's a big assumption to make.'

'I make no assumption.' Regina's tone was emphatic. 'She has no real love for him. She even refuses to give him a child!'

'You can't possibly know that,' Karen felt bound to protest.

'Then why has she not fallen pregnant in three years of marriage? Raymundo yearns for children!'

Luiz must want them too, came the thought. Or a son at least. Yet she hadn't fallen pregnant either. A failure on her part, or on his?

'It sometimes happens that way,' she said, blanking out the question. 'Three years isn't all that long.'

'It is for the Andrades. You had only been married to Luiz for four weeks when you discovered your pregnancy.' The dark eyes widened in sudden dismay at the shock expressed in the green ones opposite. 'Luiz did not tell you?'

'No.' Karen's voice seemed to be coming from a long distance away, almost drowned by the drumming in her ears. 'What happened?'

'You miscarried.' Regina was distressed, obviously at a loss as to how to proceed. 'I'm so sorry! I thought…I believed…'

It took Karen everything she had to keep herself from crumbling. A baby! She'd been going to have a baby! How could she not have known that?

'I suppose Luiz thought I had enough to deal with at present,' she got out. 'How…far gone was I?'

'Almost two months.' The distress was growing by the moment. 'He will be furious with me for telling you. How can I have been so dense?'

'I had to know some time.' Fighting to stay on top of her chaotic emotions, Karen drew a deep breath. 'Do you know what caused me to miscarry?'

'The doctors could find no organic reason for it. And they said there was no cause to fear it might happen again.' Regina was eager to repair at least some of the harm she had done. 'You will have many healthy babies, I'm sure of it!'

She broke off once more in recollection of the present circumstances, pulling a rueful face. 'I speak before I think again. Can you ever forgive me?'

Karen forced a smile. 'There's nothing to forgive.' Her hesitation was brief, the need to know outweighing the reluctance to ask. 'Did Luiz blame me for it?'

'Blame you?' Regina sounded shocked. 'Of course not! He was devastated, of course, but his concern was mostly for you. He loves you so much, Karen. You must believe that!'

'He told me we had disagreements.'

It was Regina's turn to hesitate. 'Well, yes. He can be a little imperious at times. But there was never any serious disunity, until—'

'Until I suddenly upped and went,' Karen finished for her.

The younger girl nodded. 'It was a shock to all of us, but to Luiz most of all. Whatever he'd said or done to make you do such a thing, he was utterly distraught. It was fortunate that he returned early to the house. You had been gone no longer than an hour or two when he set out after you.'

Karen's brows were drawn together in an effort to break through the barriers. 'How could he know where I was heading?' she asked, only just stopping herself from saying we.

'You had taken your passport, as if your intention was to return to England, but if so you could have gone there direct from São Paulo. I believe you went to Rio because he had made you unhappy, and you just wished to teach him a lesson.'

As a mere gesture, it would have been a little over the top, Karen reflected. Better that Regina retained the notion, though, than know the truth. Whether Lucio Fernandas would have told anyone else about the affair there was no way of knowing, although fear that Luiz would find out should surely have been enough to keep his mouth closed.

She still found the affair itself so difficult to accept. The way she felt about marital infidelity now was the way she'd always felt—the way her parents had felt. She'd read somewhere that losing a baby could affect a woman in more ways than just the physical. Was it possible that her loss had triggered a whole change of character?

'The car you took was fetched back from the airport yesterday,' Regina continued, intent on filling in the pieces for her.

Distracted, Karen said blankly, 'I can drive?'

'Of course. How else could you have got there? Luiz taught you himself. It meant we no longer had to call on Carlos. I hold a licence too now, but I'm happy to direct you.'

Karen shook her head, mind whirling. 'If I can't remember being able to drive, I can hardly just set off. I wouldn't even know *how* to change gear, much less when!'

'The car you drive is an automatic,' Regina answered, 'but I understand your reluctance. Perhaps it will come back to you quickly when you do try.'

Karen couldn't imagine it. If she knew what time Luiz might be back she would stay and face him with what she had just learned, but sitting around waiting for him to put in an appearance would only serve to increase the anger boiling up inside her. He should have told her about the baby! How could he *not* have told her? What else was he keeping from her?

'What should I wear?' she asked, desperate to stop herself from dwelling on it all. 'To go to town, I mean.'

'We dress very casually on most occasions,' Regina advised. 'Especially in the summer. You must wear what you find the most comfortable.' She gave a sigh. 'It's difficult to remember how little you know of our ways. You became so much a part of us.'

'I was never homesick?'

'Perhaps a little at times, but Luiz could soon bring a smile back to your lips. You told me once that he was the only man you had ever loved.' She glanced at the watch encircling her wrist. 'We should go while the morning is still young.'

Karen went up to her room and changed the dress

she'd slipped on for a pair of light cotton trousers and a shirt, similar to what Regina herself was wearing. The wad of notes was still in the wallet. She still had no idea of the value, but there would surely be ample should she fancy buying anything. Not that shopping was of any interest right now.

Only on opening another section did she find the platinum credit card bearing her name. She must have been relying on that as a means of obtaining more money, she thought painfully. It was more than likely that Lucio Fernandas had been relying on it too, hence the disappearing act when she was knocked down. The last thing he would have wanted was to be around when Luiz came on the scene.

The whole concept was intolerable. What spell had the man cast on her?

Fairly minor though it was, the town offered a variety of shops, restaurants and places of entertainment. Bathed in a glow of gilt, the church was a baroque magnificence. The market was held in a tree-shaded square, a collection of gaily coloured awnings covering stalls selling everything and anything.

Wandering through them at Regina's side, Karen was aware of sideways glances and whispered comments from one or two of the vendors. She did her best to ignore them. Fretting about it wouldn't help anything. She simply had to learn to live with it.

The woman Regina greeted by one of the stalls made a valiant effort to show no discomfiture. She was in her early thirties, face and figure comfortably rounded.

'This is Dona Ferrez,' said Regina. 'She and her husband, Marques, are close family friends.'

'I'm sorry to be like this,' proffered Karen with a

smile before the other could speak, determined to grasp the nettle firmly.

'The fault is far from yours,' Dona assured her in stilted English, looking a little more relaxed. 'We were all of us desolated to hear of your accident. You must be finding matters very difficult.'

'It certainly isn't easy,' Karen agreed. 'I feel like a fish out of water!'

'It would be best for you to meet with all the people who know you at the one time,' the other suggested. 'I will arrange a barbecue for this coming Sunday.'

Unable to see a way out of what threatened to be a pretty overwhelming experience, Karen could only smile and nod. 'That's very thoughtful of you. I'll look forward to it.'

'It won't be so very bad,' Regina comforted as they moved on. 'The people who will be there will be only too anxious to put you at your ease. You are regarded very highly by all our friends.'

'I've met them often?'

'On many occasions. We socialise a great deal. Unlike Rio, it can become quite cold at times here in winter. Our entertainment then takes place indoors.'

Karen had always believed Brazil to be hot everywhere all year round but, covering such a vast area, she supposed there had to be variations in climate. She preferred the idea of some seasonal change in temperature. It made it seem more like home.

Home. The wave of nostalgia that swept her was grievous. Would she ever see England again?

The desire to confront Luiz had subsided to some extent by the time they returned to the house. The sight of him lounging on the veranda, seemingly without a care in the world, brought it all surging back.

Wearing dark jeans and T-shirt, his feet clad in leather boots, he looked very different from the man who had brought her here yesterday. His working gear, she guessed, although someone in his position would hardly be called on to perform any manual labour.

'How long have you been waiting?' asked Regina a little tentatively.

'Perhaps an hour,' he said. His eyes were on Karen, appraising the spots of colour burning high on her cheekbones. 'You enjoyed the market?'

'I didn't recall anything, if that's what you really want to know,' she answered shortly.

Her tone brought a sudden narrowing of the dark eyes. 'You sound hostile,' he observed. 'Is there something you have to say to me?'

'It's my fault.' Regina looked as though she would prefer to be anywhere but where she was at this moment. 'I thought Karen knew about the baby.'

'Which I would have, if you'd had the decency to tell me about it yourself!' Karen cut in. 'Don't blame Regina for taking it for granted you would have done!'

'Regina should have had the sense to realise how far from ready you were for such a disclosure,' he returned, directing an angry glance at his sister. 'You have enough to contend with.'

'I'm the best judge of what I can or can't deal with,' Karen flashed, and saw his lips slant.

'How would you know whether or not you're able to deal with matters in advance of the information being imparted? I made the judgement I thought best for you.'

'Then stop it!' She was trembling, but too fired up to withdraw. 'If I'm to have any hope at all of regaining my memory I need to know everything there is to know about these past months. So anything else you're holding back I'd—'

'There's nothing more.' The interruption was terse. 'If there was, we would not be discussing it here and now. I think it might be best if you took some time to calm yourself before we discuss anything at all.' He held up a staying hand as she started to speak. 'I said that's enough!'

Karen subsided with reluctance, not quite up to meeting the challenge. Regina had said he could be imperious; she had certainly been right!

Maddening though she found it now, and would almost certainly have found it then, she doubted all the same if it would have been enough on its own to send her careering into another man's arms. There *had* to be something more! Something he still wasn't telling her.

A flicker of movement from the doorway drew her eyes. Whoever had been standing there had gone, but she had a strong feeling that it had been Beatriz. If what Regina had told her was to be taken seriously, the woman's dislike of her was easier to understand, if not appreciate. She felt sorry for Raymundo.

'I think I might go and lie down for an hour,' she said, suddenly weary of it all.

Luiz inclined his head, his expression giving little away. 'By all means.'

'You will come down for lunch?' asked Regina. 'We eat at two.'

It was only just twelve. 'I'll be there,' Karen confirmed, more to please her sister-in-law than through any desire for food.

She made her escape before anything else could be said. Gaining the bedroom, she stood for a moment or two trying to gather herself. The weariness was more mental than physical. She felt totally drained.

There was little comfort to be gained by lying down. Sleep had never seemed further away. She put her hands to her smooth abdomen, still finding it difficult to believe that she'd carried a child for two months. Had it been a boy or a girl? Had she miscarried here, or in hospital? The questions kept piling up, whirling like dervishes around her brain. There was so much she needed to know.

The gentle knock on the door came as some relief. Regina might be in the dark regarding the reason she had left Guavada, but she could provide at least one or two more answers.

Except that it wasn't Regina who came into the room at her invitation, but Luiz himself, tautening her throat afresh.

'I came to apologise,' he said unexpectedly. 'I should have warned Regina to keep her own counsel on the matter until you were better able to withstand the shock. The blame is mine, not hers. I can only hope you suffer no lasting harm from learning the news so precipitately.'

Propped on an elbow, Karen regarded the firmly controlled features with eyes suddenly opened to the realisation that she wasn't the only one who'd undergone the loss. His loss, in fact, was twofold: not just his child, but his wife too.

'It can't have been easy for you either at the time,' she said softly.

The dark head inclined. 'No, it was not—though the assurance that there was no reason to fear it happening again was some consolation.'

'Did we try for another baby?' Karen ventured.

'No. I believed it best to take a little time to ourselves first. If I'd realised...' He broke off, jaw tensing. 'What can't be altered must be endured.'

'If you believe I began this affair with Lucio Fernandas some way back, it seems odd that Beatriz was the only one to suspect anything,' Karen got out with difficulty.

'The two of you were obviously very circumspect in your meetings. Beatriz herself became suspicious only a matter of days before you left.'

'I'd have thought she would have tried to warn you.'

The shrug was dismissive. 'If she had, I might have thought she was simply attempting to cause trouble between us. She never approved of the marriage.'

Considering what Regina had told her earlier, Karen could understand that. What she still couldn't understand was how on earth she and this Lucio had managed to keep the affair so secret. If it weren't for the fact that Luiz had verified the names on the passenger list to Rio that day, she might even suspect Beatriz of making the whole thing up in order to discredit her in his eyes.

'I'm sorry,' she proffered miserably. 'I know I keep saying that, but it's all I *can* say. I hate to think of what I've done to you—to our marriage. I only wish I could somehow put things right again.'

Dark eyes travelled the length of her body, revealing a hunger that stirred her to the depths. When he moved it was with purpose, coming across to sit down on the edge of the bed and draw her up into his arms.

Karen met the kiss hesitantly at first, not at all sure if this was what she wanted right now: a hesitancy dispersed in seconds by the emotions sweeping through her. Her arms lifted of their own accord to slide about his neck, her fingers tangling in the crisp thickness. Her breasts were pressed against the hardness of his chest, springing the nipples to vibrant life, her nostrils filled with the male scent of him. There was a dampness between her thighs, an aching need she could barely sustain. If her mind failed to recall what fulfilment felt like, her body had no such problem.

Without removing his lips from hers, Luiz reached between them to unbutton her shirt, sliding his hand inside to seek the firm curve of her breast. Karen caught her breath as his fingers enclosed the sensitive, tingling tip, moaning deep in her throat at a sensation so close to pain yet so infinitely pleasurable.

She was bereft when he withdrew the hand and put her from him to rise abruptly to his feet again.

'I'll show you round the ranch after lunch,' he said without looking at her. 'I have other matters to attend to for now.'

Karen eased herself to a sitting position as the door closed behind him, reaching with numbed fingers to fasten the buttons he had opened. She had wanted him to make love to her so badly, but the spectre of Lucio Fernandas still loomed too large. Perhaps there would come a time when he was able to put the images that haunted him from his mind. If they were to make anything at all of this marriage of theirs, he would have to. They would both have to.

Beatriz was missing from the lunch table. She had gone to visit a friend, Raymundo advised. Karen could only be grateful for the woman's absence. There were questions only Beatriz could answer for her, but she was reluctant to ask them for fear of what she might hear.

Whatever Luiz had been feeling earlier, he appeared to have recovered from it. Conversation was light throughout the meal. Regina greeted the news that he was to take Karen on a tour of the ranch with pleasure, obviously reassured that things were working out between them.

They went by Jeep, to Karen's relief. She had never, to the best of her knowledge, ridden a horse in her life. The corrals she had originally expected to see lay some half a mile from the house, backed by barns and other outbuildings. There were several ranch hands around employed on various jobs. Luiz stopped to speak with one of them who appeared to be in charge, leaving Karen to fidget beneath the covert glances cast by those in the vicinity.

If Lucio Fernandas had lived and worked with these men it seemed unlikely that none of them had known of his affair with the wife of their employer, yet it seemed equally unlikely that if any of them *had* known they would have kept totally quiet about it. Her memory loss would be the reason for the glances. There probably wasn't a solitary soul within a hundred mile radius who hadn't heard about *that*!

'I'm beginning to feel a regular freak,' she commented wryly when they were on their way again. 'It was the same in town this morning. Everyone staring and whispering!'

'It will soon be forgotten,' Luiz answered, giving way to a smile at the realisation of what he'd just said. 'An unfortunate turn of phrase in the circumstances.'

Karen smiled too, heartened by the humour. 'But hopefully true.' She paused, looking for some non-contentious subject. 'We met someone called Dona Ferrez in town this morning. She offered to arrange a barbecue on Sunday in order for me to get all the meetings over with at the one time.'

'Thoughtful of her.' Luiz directed a glance. 'How do you feel about it?'

'Nervous,' she admitted. 'But there's no point crying off. At least none of them...'

'None of them will know why you were in Rio to begin with,' Luiz supplied levelly as she let the words peter out. 'A question I may be called on to answer myself.'

'You could say I was shopping,' she suggested after a moment, and saw his lips twist.

'There's nothing you could buy in Rio that couldn't be obtained in São Paulo city, but then, there's no accounting for a woman's whim.'

He brought the Jeep to a halt as a party of riders appeared round a bend in the trail. The leader approached the vehicle without dismounting, his attitude respectful. A good-looking man in his thirties, lithe and fit in his working gear of denims and shirt, much like those Luiz himself had been wearing earlier.

Karen kept her eyes front as the two men conversed. If this man was the ranch foreman, as seemed likely, he had been the one to employ Lucio Fernandas. Obviously, Luiz accorded him no blame. But then why should he? The man could hardly have foretold what was to happen.

'I think I'd like to go back now,' she said dully when the men departed. 'I have a headache coming on.'

It was no out and out lie, though Luiz's immediate solicitude made her feel guilty of deception.

'Of course,' he said. 'I should have realised that the Jeep would prove too jolting a ride for you.'

The Jeep had nothing to do with what was ailing her, but it sufficed as an excuse. Karen closed her eyes as he turned back along the track, hoping he would take the hint and not attempt to talk. She felt so utterly debased.

Luiz despatched her to rest again when they reached the house. She went without protest, needing some time alone to try pulling herself together.

The dull ache behind her eyes was no aid to clear thinking. Not that clarity of thought had any bearing when it came to pondering the imponderable. While her mind refused to release the memory of these past months she had to accept the situation as it appeared, regardless of how much she deplored it.

She was sitting at the window watching the sun slowly sink beneath the horizon when a knock came at the door. Expecting Luiz, she was surprised to see Beatriz enter the room in answer to her invitation.

The older woman closed the door and stood with her back to it, gazing hard-faced across the distance between them.

'What do you hope to gain by this act?' she demanded harshly.

'It's no act.' Karen was hard put to keep her voice from revealing her inner turbulence. 'I don't remember anything that happened these past months. Why should you doubt it?'

'Because I know how devious you are,' came the taut reply. 'If you hope…'

She broke off, biting her lip as if about to say something she hadn't planned on saying. 'Luiz was a fool for ever marrying you!' she spat.

'It was probably a foolish move on both our parts.' Karen drew a steadying breath, reluctant to ask the question yet unable to refrain from it too. 'Luiz tells me you suspected I was…seeing Lucio Fernandas.'

The expression that flickered across the other face was difficult to define in the lowering light. When the answer came it was in a subtly altered tone. 'Yes.'

'So why didn't you tell him?'

The pause was brief. 'Because I had no proof and feared his reaction. I had no choice but to tell him when you left.' Her tone hardened again. 'He should have let you go! You were never worthy to hold the name of Andrade!'

'So it seems.' Karen made a valiant effort to hang on to some semblance of self-respect. 'Unfortunately, Luiz doesn't believe in divorce.'

'But neither can he keep you here against your will.'

The light was almost gone. Karen reached out a hand to the table at her side and switched on the reading lamp, gazing across at her sister-in-law with drawn brows.

'You're suggesting I should leave again anyway?'

'The only honourable course,' came the answer. 'How can Luiz be expected to feel anything but disgust for you after what you did? What kind of life are you condemning him to by staying?'

'What kind of life would *I* have to look forward to if I did as you say?' Karen asked, doing her best to stay in control of her emotions. 'I've no home, no job. I'm not even sure I have enough, if any, money of my own left to get me back home to start with.'

'I could help you there.'

The offer came too pat to be anything but premeditated. Swept by a disgust of her own, Karen got to her feet, better to face the woman.

'For what purpose?' she shot back. 'Divorced or not, Luiz would never turn to you for solace.' She shook her head emphatically as Beatriz made to speak. 'This has gone far enough. I want you to leave. And in case there's any doubt left in your mind, *I'll* be staying.'

The striking features opposite were for a moment suffused with a fury that turned them almost ugly, tawny eyes glittering with hatred. When she moved it was abruptly, the door slamming in her wake.

Karen sank back into the seat she had vacated, the anger that had driven her to her feet overridden by shame that she had allowed herself to be goaded into retaliation.

Tomorrow was Saturday. The best time to catch Julie at home—once she'd discovered what the time difference between here and London was. Reluctant though she felt to put the question, she had to know what her friend might have been told. Only if she heard it from Julie's lips could she really start to believe there had been an affair.

CHAPTER FIVE

TIME differences in Brazil apparently differed by region. São Paulo was only three hours behind GMT, Luiz advised at dinner when asked. If she rang around eleven in the morning, she'd catch Julie at breakfast, Karen calculated. In the meantime, there was another night to be got through.

Luiz made no move to accompany her when she took her leave barely an hour after they finished eating. He seemed distant. Hardly to be wondered at, Karen supposed. He was still having difficulty coming to terms with their altered circumstances. How long it might be before he managed to set the knowledge of her apparent betrayal aside was anyone's guess. It might be never. Only if she could prove that there was no truth in it did they stand a chance of restoring all they'd lost—and how did she do that when all *she* had to go on was instinct?

She was still awake when he came to bed himself; she heard the movement from the next room. She'd tried the connecting door earlier and found it now unlocked, but she doubted if he had been the one to do the unlocking. Regina, at a guess. Her young sister-in-law would probably try anything to get the two of them together again.

A part of her wanted desperately to get up and go to him, but the fear of rejection was stronger. It had to be up to him to make the first move. For now, all she could do was deal with the need churning her whole body as best she may.

Morning brought rain. A downpour that lasted more than an hour and stopped as suddenly as it had begun. Viewing the still heavy skies from the veranda after breakfast, Karen wondered if there was more to come.

'It will clear,' Luiz told her. 'In a little while the sun will break through and the land will begin to steam. At least here the humidity remains at a bearable level. Rio is like a sauna in the rain.'

'It was bad enough even without it,' Karen returned, recalling the impact when she'd emerged into the open for the first time back at the clinic. 'I can't imagine how anyone manages to work in that kind of heat!'

'The offices are air-conditioned, the ones who work outdoors are accustomed to it,' he said. 'Do you plan to telephone your friend today?'

'As soon as I think she'll be up and about.' Karen stole a glance at him, uncertain of his mood. 'You don't object?'

The bronzed features remained impassive. 'Why should I object? Perhaps she will be able to shed some light on your memory.'

Having given the possibility some thought overnight, Karen doubted that she would have told Julie she'd been having an affair, in the certain knowledge of what her friend's reaction would be. All she could hope for was that there might be something Julie *could* tell her that would fire a spark.

The rest of the family had dispersed, leaving the two of them alone. Beatriz had had little to say for herself this morning, though her attitude certainly hadn't altered. Karen dismissed the woman from her mind. Right now, she had more important concerns.

Seated in one of the lounging chairs, legs thrust out before him, Luiz looked relaxed on the surface, but she could sense the tension in him. He was dressed casually in lightweight trousers and cotton shirt.

'Are you free all day today?' she asked tentatively.

'I'm free whenever I wish it,' he answered. 'My foremen need no supervision.' His head turned her way, gaze sliding over her face to linger for a heart-thudding moment on the vulnerable curve of her mouth. 'Your injuries are fading fast. Not that they could detract from your beauty even at their worst. I can blame no man for wanting you, but I'll kill any other who attempts to take you from me—as I would Lucio Fernandas should I ever catch up with him.'

The tone was almost conversational. Only in the depths of the dark eyes did the ferocity show. Karen drew a shallow breath.

'If I chose to have an affair with him, then the fault is just as much mine.'

'You say *if*?' Luiz's tone had hardened. 'For what other reason would the two of you have been travelling together? For what other reason would you have left at all?'

'I don't know,' she said wretchedly. 'According to what you told me back in the hospital, everything appeared normal with our marriage right up until the night before I left, but I'm sure it wouldn't have been if I'd been…sleeping with another man.'

'Meaning you would have been unable to respond to me physically?' Luiz slanted a lip. 'You give me little credit.'

Karen felt warmth rise under her skin beneath the sardonic gaze, a stirring deep in the pit of her stomach. Whatever the circumstances, he would have no difficulty at all in arousing her. He was doing it now without even trying, making her yearn for what she couldn't even remember.

'I meant in other ways,' she got out. 'There must have been *something*!'

The hesitation was brief. 'You've seemed withdrawn at times these last weeks, I admit. I assumed the moodiness was due both to the loss you'd suffered and the normal female cycle, but perhaps I was simply deluding myself.' He straightened abruptly, getting to his feet. 'Whichever, it's past and gone. What we have to deal with is the present. I'll leave you to make your call.'

It wasn't nearly time, she could have said, but she refrained, reluctant though she was to be left with only her thoughts for company. She watched him stride indoors, feeling the fast-becoming-familiar contraction in the region of her groin at the supple movement of his hard-packed thighs. The hunger in her owed nothing to memory, everything to instinct. She ached in every fibre.

She was still aching when Raymundo joined her some twenty minutes or so later, dropping into the chair vacated by his brother.

'You should not be left alone to brood,' he said. 'Not in your condition.'

Karen turned a blank look. 'Condition?'

'Your memory loss. It must be difficult for you.'

'It has to be difficult for everyone,' she returned, following it up with a faint smile. 'Apart from Regina. She won't allow it to be.'

'My sister adored you from the moment you arrived at Guavada,' he claimed extravagantly. 'As did everyone.'

Karen allowed herself an edge of sarcasm. 'Everyone?'

Raymundo gave a wry shrug. 'Sadly, my wife allows jealousy to impair her judgement. Until your arrival, she was the…'

'Queen bee?' Karen supplied as he hesitated over the term.

His smile was a little discomfited. 'Mistress of the household, I believe you would call it. Handing over that charge to you was hard for her.'

'She must have known Luiz would marry some day,' Karen protested, wondering if Raymundo could possibly be as blind to his wife's true feelings as Regina had made out.

'But perhaps to someone content to allow things to stay the same.'

'Which I obviously wasn't.'

The smile came again, wry this time. 'No. Nor, I think, would Luiz have been happy had you been. He loved your spirit as well as your beauty. He…'

He broke off, shaking his head in rueful recollection. 'I speak in the past tense. Luiz loves you still, I'm sure of it.'

'I take it Beatriz made no mention of her suspicions to you either?' Karen said after a moment.

'No.' He looked discomfited again. 'She told no one until Luiz found you gone. He was angry with her for keeping it from him, but all she had was suspicion.'

'Odd, that no one else appears to have had any notion.'

'Women are renowned for their intuition,' he said with a certain reserve.

Karen left it there, sensing that she wasn't going to get any further. The more she heard, the more she suspected that Beatriz might have somehow set her up. Proving it was another matter, but at the very least it gave her some hope.

Dubious though she was that Julie could be of any help, she still needed to speak to her. She was the only contact she had with home. It was only half past ten, but she could wait no longer.

'I have to make a phone call,' she said, getting up. 'Can I dial direct to England?'

'Providing you know your country code,' Raymundo confirmed. 'You may have some difficulty getting through. The lines are often busy.'

'I'll manage.'

She made her escape, heading back indoors. She reached her bedroom without running into anyone, closing the door before crossing to the telephone on the bedside table. So far as memory went, she'd last spoken to Julie the day before she'd woken up in the hospital. In reality, she had no idea just how long it had been.

As Raymundo had warned, it took a little time and effort to get the call through. Even when the connection was made, an age seemed to pass before the receiver was lifted. The voice on the other end of the line sounded sleepy.

'Can't a body have a lie in on a Saturday morning, for heaven's sake? It's not even eight!'

'Julie, it's me,' Karen said swiftly. 'Sorry about the time.'

'That's okay.' She sounded wide awake now, though still far from her normal vibrant self. 'How are you, Karen? It's been ages! My fault mostly, I have to admit. I changed my job. Just never got round to answering your last call. Anyway, how's it going? Still madly in love with that gorgeous Brazilian hunk?'

'Of course.' It was all Karen could say. It was obvious that she'd passed nothing at all on to the other girl, which meant there was little to be gained from telling her about her memory loss, with all the subsequent explanations. 'I just thought I'd give you a call,' she tagged on lamely. 'I must have miscalculated the time difference.'

'You're forgiven.' Julie was fast recovering from the guilt she apparently felt over her tardiness in making contact. 'What's the weather like over there? It's raining cats and dogs here!'

'Fine.' The last thing Karen felt like was an exchange of weather details. 'A good move, was it, the new job?'

'Sure was! I've met the most wonderful man! Not a patch on your Luiz, of course, but it's given to few of us to be quite *that* lucky in love! I must say, I thought you'd gone utterly mad when you rang to say you were never coming back, but then I thought you were utterly mad spending all your winnings on a trip to Rio in the first place. I'm just so glad it's all turned out so well.'

There was a pause, as if in anticipation of some response, a slight change of tone. 'Everything *is* all right, isn't it?'

If there had been any hesitation left in Karen's mind, it was banished now. 'Of course,' she said. 'Couldn't be better! I'm really happy you've found someone yourself, Julie. I hope it works out.'

The two of them chatted a while longer about general matters, parting on the promise to keep in more regular contact from now on. Karen replaced the receiver with a heavy heart, suspecting that the friendship would continue to slide. Not that she blamed Julie for neglecting to call. She had her own life to lead: a very full one, by all accounts.

What *she* had to concentrate on now was attempting to rebuild the relationship she'd destroyed by running away—whatever her reason for doing it. According to Raymundo, Luiz still loved her, but how could he know that? Luiz was unlikely to have confided his innermost feelings.

Without proof, there was no way she was going to convince him that there had been no affair; she couldn't be wholly convinced herself, if it came to that. So all she could do was try to wipe out the hurt. If that meant putting her pride on the line and risking rebuff, then so be it. One way or another, she was going to get this marriage back on track.

She went through the day in a fever of anticipation mingled with apprehension. The way Luiz made her feel, there was no physical barrier: desire, it seemed, transcended memory loss. She wanted his lovemaking, wanted desperately to be reminded of how it felt to be nude in his arms, to have his hands exploring her body, his lips seeking hers.

Just how deep her feelings had gone, there was no way of knowing, though it seemed unlikely that she'd have married him for sex alone, however wonderful.

On the other hand, even if her suspicions regarding the supposed affair turned out to be right, she still had to find a reason why she had left him.

She was getting nowhere with this, Karen decided wryly. If she didn't want to drive herself mad, she had to put the whole thing aside and start again from here.

With both Beatriz and Raymundo out for the evening, dinner was a more relaxed occasion—or would have been if she hadn't been on tenterhooks over her plans for later. The temptation to shelve everything and wait for Luiz himself to make another approach was great.

Keyed up, she knocked over her water glass, cascading liquid across the table.

'You seem tense,' Luiz remarked when the mopping up was done and order restored. 'Is your head troubling you again?'

'No, it's fine,' Karen assured him. 'I was just clumsy, that's all.'

'I've done the same thing myself on occasion,' chimed in Regina. 'At least it was only water.' She gave a girlish giggle. 'I once tipped a whole glass of red wine over a guest. She was most annoyed.'

'Understandably,' her brother returned drily. 'Her clothing was ruined.'

'Only because she refused to allow me to practise the remedy I read about and throw white wine over the stains,' came the unperturbed reply. 'One is supposed to bleach out the other. Have you heard of that, Karen?'

'Actually, yes,' Karen agreed. 'Although I can't say I've ever tried it.' She smiled at the younger girl, grateful for the intervention she suspected was designed to switch Luiz's attention. 'We'll have to experiment some time just in case.'

'What time shall we be expected at this barbecue tomorrow?' she added, looking for more diversion.

'Any time from noon onwards,' Regina answered. 'People arrive when they feel like it. The food will be cooking all day. You must not worry about seeing everyone. They will all do their utmost, I'm sure, to be at ease with you.'

Easier said than done from both sides, Karen reflected. Rather worse for herself, considering she would have a whole lot of names to fit to faces. Hopefully, everyone would speak at least some English, because her grasp of Portuguese showed little sign of returning as yet.

She could feel Luiz's eyes on her, penetrating her defences. Without glancing in his direction, she was vitally aware of his lean length, his breadth of shoulder and depth of chest. The tailored trousers he was wearing enclosed the essence of his masculinity: the part of him that had been a part of her, that had sown the seed from which the baby she had lost had begun to grow. It felt so strange to know that yet have no physiological concept of it.

Once again, Luiz simply said goodnight when she announced her intention of retiring around eleven. Karen went to her room still in a state of flux. It was only a bare four days since she had woken up to all this in the clinic. There was no denying the desire Luiz aroused in her, but was it enough on its own? Had it ever been enough?

While reluctant to believe that she might have married him on the crest of that particular wave, the possibility had to be faced that it was the lack of any deeper emotion that had caused her to make a break for freedom.

That the same reason might be given for seeking an affair was something she refused to contemplate. Whatever Lucio Fernandas had been doing on that plane, he hadn't been with her, she was certain of it.

She was in bed, though far from sleep, when Luiz

entered the next room. She lay listening to the faint sounds, waiting for the silence that would tell her he was in bed himself.

Even then, it was another half an hour before she finally forced her limbs into movement, closing her mind to the misgivings. Something had to be done; they couldn't go on like this. If she hadn't loved him with any depth before, she could learn to do it now. In three short months, she'd hardly given it a chance.

She eased the door open as quietly as possible. The room beyond was in darkness, the bed on the far side lit only by a stray gleam of moonlight. Karen hesitated on the threshold, fighting the urge to turn back. She stifled a gasp when Luiz rolled over and sat up.

'What is it?' he asked. 'Are you ill?'

'No.' Her voice sounded thick. 'I thought...I wanted...' She drew in another breath as he put out an arm with the obvious intention of reaching for a lamp switch. 'Don't put the light on, please!'

His arm fell back. Highlighting the white linen sheet covering the lower half of his body, the moonlight left the rest of him in shadow. Only when he leaned forward a little did she see that he was naked from at least the waist up. Eyes adjusting, she viewed the dark curls of hair across his chest with a leap in an already racing pulse rate, feeling her nipples peak in what could only be anticipation.

'You wanted?' he prompted after a moment.

'You,' she said before she could lose it altogether. 'I want *you*, Luiz!'

There was no immediate reaction. His skin looked like oiled silk in the moonlight. Face still partially shadowed, he gazed across at her. When he did speak it was in low, controlled tones.

'Why?'

Karen's mind grappled with the unexpected question. Surely the answer was obvious.

'Because it's driving me crazy!' she burst out. 'Because I can't bear another minute of feeling the way you make me feel without doing something about it! I realise how difficult it must be for you believing I've been with another man, and I know you're not going to believe me when I say *I* know I haven't.'

'*How* do you know?'

'I just do,' she said. 'Call it instinct. Call it what you like.'

The pause was lengthy, his expression—what she could see of it—giving nothing away. 'You're suggesting that Beatriz was lying?' he said at length.

About to confirm, Karen bit the words back, settling for a compromise instead. 'Or simply mistaken.'

'Then how would you explain Fernandas's name on the passenger list?'

'I can't,' she admitted. 'I can't explain what *I* was doing on that plane, much less him! I suppose it's possible we'll never know, but if I'm to stay here—'

'There's no question of anything other,' came the harsh interruption.

Karen spread her hands. 'Fine. I accept that. Only we both have to make the effort to put things right between us. If you turn me down now…'

'You think me capable of it?'

He threw back the sheet, revealing his nudity all the way down. He was already fully and heart-jerkingly aroused. Karen felt her stomach muscles contract, the heat rush through her.

'You're right,' he said on a softer note. 'Our only recourse is to wipe the past from mind. Come.'

Heart thudding like a trip hammer, every nerve-ending in her body on fire, she reached the bed.

'Take off your gown,' Luiz instructed, still in the same tone. 'Let me see you.'

Karen reached for the thin straps with fingers that felt nerveless, sliding them down over her shoulders to let the heavy silk glide to the floor at her feet. She felt no reticence in revealing herself to him, only gratification at the look she saw in the eyes scanning every inch of her body.

He said something in his own language, the words foreign to her ears yet somehow understandable. When he held out a hand to her, she went willingly into his arms.

She had longed to feel those supple hands of his on her body, and he left no part of her untouched. She writhed in ecstasy beneath his caresses, opening herself to him with a wantonness she would never have believed herself capable of, clutching in a frenzy of sensation at the lowered dark head as he penetrated her innermost being.

She felt no reticence either in returning the caresses, pressing lingering, teasing kisses down the muscular length of him to bring him almost to the point of climax with the wicked use of tongue and teeth.

When he finally turned her under him, her legs wrapped themselves almost of their own accord about his hips, her whole body arching to the incredible feel of him sliding inside her, carrying her with him on a roller coaster ride to sheer heaven. She climaxed only a bare moment before he did, her cries mingling with his deep down groans.

'Has it always been like that between us?' she whispered when she could speak at all, hardly able to believe her own overwhelming passion.

Luiz lifted his head, eyes fathomless pools in the dim light. 'Perhaps not quite the same.'

'Meaning you had to teach me how to…respond?'

'Only in the sense of releasing you from the inhibitions covering your true nature.' He lifted a hand to smooth the tumbled damp hair back from her face, lingering to caress the smooth line of her cheek. 'The first time I took you was an experience I will never forget. You were so anxious to please me, so apologetic for your lack of experience, so unaware of what it means to a man to be the first to make love to a woman. You offered me your beautiful tempting lips to kiss, your lovely body to do with as I would.'

'When did you decide you wanted to marry me?' Karen murmured.

He gave a brief smile. 'I was captivated for life the moment I set eyes on you.'

'You really would have wanted to marry me even if I hadn't proved to be a virgin?'

'As I already told you on Corcovado, yes. The virginity was, as the Americans would say, the icing on the cake.'

'You're American yourself,' she said.

'*South* American,' he corrected. 'A world of difference!' His tone softened again as if in reminiscence. 'I only discovered your lack of experience when you revealed it in fear that you would be unable to satisfy me.'

Karen was silent for a moment or two, trying to break through the fog in her mind, giving up because it was a hopeless exercise. She brought her own hand up to lightly trace the lips that had given her so much pleasure, registering the desire building in her again without surprise. Whether what she felt for this man had been more than just a physical need before her memory loss, she still couldn't say, but what she was feeling right now surely went beyond it.

'There's no way I could ever have turned to another man while I had you!' she declared with passion. 'You have to believe it, Luiz!'

'We agreed to put the matter aside,' he returned on a resolute note. 'Until your memory returns, there is no other way.'

If it didn't return the question would never be answered, whispered a treacherous little voice at the back of her mind. Affair or no affair, *something* had moved her into taking flight.

She blanked the thought out as Luiz bent his lips to hers once more.

It was apparent from the way Regina regarded the two of them at breakfast that she had noted a difference in attitude this morning. Judging from the looks Beatriz directed their way, she was aware of it too, and not at all happy about it.

Karen forced herself to ignore the glances. She and Luiz might only have achieved a partial reconciliation last night, but it was a vital part. Recovering her memory could even be a bad thing in the long run, came the thought. What she didn't know couldn't hurt her.

'I must get down to learning the language again,' she declared. 'I obviously didn't find it too difficult before.' She gave a laugh. 'I bet I'm one of the few people to have to do it twice!'

'Very possibly the only one,' Luiz returned. 'You may even find your ear already attuned.'

'I'll help all I can,' offered Regina eagerly. 'Good morning is *bom dia*, good afternoon *boa tarde*, although you—'

'I think Karen may have already worked out the basics for herself,' her brother interjected drily.

Regina lowered her head, the quirk of her lips belying the apparent humility. '*Desculpe*,' she murmured. '*Me perdoe*, Karen.'

'There's nothing to be sorry for,' Karen answered, taking a guess at the meaning. 'Any help at all is welcome.'

'I was just going to say that you need no formal address to greet people who already know you,' her sister-in-law returned, casting a sly glance in Luiz's direction. '*Oi* will be sufficient.'

Meaning hello, Karen surmised, doubtful if she could produce quite the same sound. She still felt daunted at the thought of meeting these people Regina was speaking of, but it had to be done. At least none of them would be aware of what she'd really been doing in Rio.

She shelved *that* thought before it could get going.

Neither Raymundo nor Beatriz showed any interest in attending the barbecue. Karen felt more than a little impatient with her brother-in-law, who seemed totally under his wife's thumb. The antithesis of Luiz in character if not in looks.

The Ferrez home was a sprawling, single-storey villa set in grounds which for the most part appeared to have been left to prolific nature. There were already a dozen or more people there when the three of them arrived, the women dressed casually in shorts and sun tops as Regina had advised Karen to dress.

There was some awkwardness, but Karen had expected that. It was impossible for anyone to face a situation such as this with equanimity. She had mingled with these people for three months—had no doubt been hostess to similar gatherings at Guavada—yet not one face or name meant anything to her. Not everyone spoke English either, which didn't help.

Luiz stayed close at first. She did her best to cope when one of the men stole him from her side to discuss some matter or other, but she could feel the panic building inside her. These people were total strangers to her. How could she be expected to handle the situation on her own? Half the time she didn't even understand what they were saying!

In danger of losing what composure she still retained, she sought a few minutes respite in a quiet corner of the gardens. The sky was clear overhead, though cloud was gathering on the horizon. She found a seat on a stone bench, lifting her face to the sun, eyes closed against the glare. Her head felt as if it were packed with cotton wool.

'You have no drink,' said a voice.

Karen opened her eyes again with reluctance to view the man holding a wine bottle and two glasses. He had, she assumed, followed her. She sought her immediate memory for a name. Jorge Arroyo, if she had it right. Around Luiz's age, and good looking in a flashy way, he had struck her as a man with a pretty high opinion of himself. A man Luiz himself had little time for, she'd gathered.

'I've had enough to drink, thanks,' she declined. 'I just needed a little time on my own.'

The hint went unheeded. 'I sympathise with you,' he said. 'Even more so with Luiz. He was the envy of us all when he first brought you here, but he would, I think, as soon have lost you to another man than be cast so completely from mind.'

Convinced for a heart-jerking moment that he was referring to Lucio Fernandas, Karen only just stopped herself from blurting out a denial. She was hearing innuendo where none existed, she thought wryly.

'At least we're still together,' she said.

'But can it ever be the same for you?'

She lifted her shoulders, trying to keep a level head. 'As I can't remember what it was like before, that's hardly a question I can answer. Your English is excellent,' she added in an effort to steer him away from personal probing.

'We were able to converse in Portuguese just a short time ago,' he returned. 'The mind plays strange tricks.'

The 'we' disturbed her in its intimation that the two of them had shared many such conversations. There was something about the man that roused an instinctive wariness.

Luiz emerged from the shrubbery, taking in the little scene in one rapier glance.

'I've been searching for you,' he said tautly. 'Have you eaten?'

Karen shook her head, aware of his anger, and resenting it. 'Not yet.'

'Then you'll come now.'

She got to her feet, casting an uncomfortable glance in passing at the man who might not be there at all for what notice Luiz was taking of him.

'Why did you leave the others?' he demanded as they headed back along the path.

'I needed a respite,' she answered, equally shortly.

'Jorge followed you?'

Karen winged a glance at the set features, reluctant

to go on the defensive yet sensing a need to clarify the situation. 'I didn't ask him to accompany me, if that's what you're thinking.' She hesitated a moment before adding, 'Do you have something specific against him, or is it just a general antipathy?'

'It's enough for you to know that he isn't a man to be trusted,' was the short response.

She was going to get no more than that for certain, Karen acknowledged. She wasn't sure she wanted to know more anyway.

If anyone else had noted her absence, nothing was said. Food was both plentiful and excellent, the steaks the biggest she'd ever seen. She wondered if the meat came from Guavada.

'Most goes for export,' Luiz confirmed when she asked. 'But yes, we supply the surrounding areas. There's a small abattoir in the town.' Her involuntary wince drew a dry smile. 'A fact of life. The meat apart, the very sandals you're wearing owe their existence to animal hide.'

'I know,' she said. 'I know it's silly to be squeamish about it too, but I—'

'But the English love of animals extends itself to all species.' He paused a moment, viewing her with enigmatic eyes. 'Perhaps you'd like a pet of your own?'

Conscious of the tension still existing between them, she was taken aback by the offer. 'I'd love a dog,' she admitted. 'My parents always had one.'

'Then I'll see what can be arranged. Although you would have to teach it to stay away from the river. Alligators make no exceptions.'

'If there are alligators in the river, I'll make darn sure *I* stay away from it,' she said with feeling, realising just how much she had to relearn about her life here. 'What else do I need to look out for?'

'Cougars, rattlesnakes.' Luiz smiled again briefly at the look on her face. 'I tease you. Few people are faced with any heart-racing encounters.'

A foot lifted casually to rest on the edge of a wooden flower tub, shorts drawn taut across muscular thigh, he was heart-racing enough himself. Karen felt desire rising in her. She wished they were alone. Only then might they stand a chance of recapturing last night's togetherness.

'I think it's time we went home,' he said on a softer note.

Suggesting that he recognised her need was clear to him. That he was ready to set aside whatever doubts he still entertained to indulge his own need was also apparent. Not that she had any intention of denying either of them.

'What about Regina?' she asked.

'Someone will bring her.'

Dona Ferrez made no protests over their early departure, accepting Karen's plea of tiredness at face value. They had travelled here in the spacious leather-upholstered saloon that had brought them from the airport so few days ago. Head cradled against the rest as they headed back through the town, Karen contemplated the coming hour or two with growing fervour. Whatever else was missing from the marriage, nothing could take this away from them. Nothing!

CHAPTER SIX

WHILE the amnesia showed no sign of lifting in the main, Karen found herself picking up the basics of the language a great deal faster than she would have anticipated. Brazilian Portuguese was different from the European version. It was enriched by local Indian dialects, as well as African languages brought over in the past by slaves.

'Did I ever manage to get my tongue round the vowels?' she asked Luiz one evening, frustrated by her efforts to produce the right sound.

'Not quite,' he admitted. 'But it will come in time.' His expression had darkened a fraction. 'Everything becomes easier in time.'

Apart from the one thing they could neither of them put completely aside, Karen acknowledged.

'It might have been better for both of us if I'd never won that money,' she said wryly. 'If we'd never met.'

Luiz shook his head. 'I see no use in speculation of that kind. What we have, we live with.'

Brushing her hair at the dressing table, Karen watched him in the mirror as he slid into the bed. He always slept in the nude, and insisted that she did too. Not that she objected.

They'd made love every one of the past ten nights. Tonight would be no exception. Her period had to be due some time soon, she realised. It had always been around the middle of the month—although pregnancy might have altered her cycle.

Luiz hadn't mentioned the subject again, and she'd hesitated to bring it up herself. She wondered who the baby would have looked like. Had it been a boy or a girl?

Pregnancy. It was the first time she'd given a thought to the fact that Luiz never used any form of protection—and she certainly didn't. The brush suspended in mid-stroke, she considered the implications, her emotions too confused to be separated.

Propped against the pillows now, Luiz eyed her speculatively.

'Is there something you have to say?'

Her voice sounded husky. 'You think another baby would bring us closer again?'

'I think it could do no harm,' he returned without missing a stroke. 'There's no physical reason to wait.'

'We could have discussed it,' she said. 'You'd no right to make that decision on your own!'

Expression enigmatic, he said, 'You don't want a child?'

She caught herself up, biting her lip. 'That's not the point.'

'Then what is?'

'This whole situation!'

'The situation is what we make of it from now,' he returned. 'We agreed to a fresh start. Are you saying you no longer want that?'

'Of course I'm not! I just…' She broke off, lifting her shoulders in a wry shrug. 'I think it might be better to wait a while, that's all.'

'I disagree.' The tone was unequivocal. 'Are you coming to bed?'

Anger flared in her, jerking the words from her lips. 'Not just to provide you with a son and heir!'

She regretted it the moment she'd said it. Luiz hadn't moved, but his silence spoke volumes. She flung down the brush and got up to go to him, sinking down on the bed edge to lay her cheek against his chest. 'That was unfair,' she whispered.

He slid a hand into her hair to caress the nape of her neck, but she could feel the rigidity in him. 'If you don't feel ready,' he said.

'I do.' She lifted her head to look at him, putting everything she had into convincing herself as well as him. 'I want us to get back to where we were in the beginning. Anyway,' she added, trying for a lighter note, 'it could already be an accomplished fact. No use shutting the stable door after the horse has bolted!'

The smile that curved his lips failed to strike an answering spark in his eyes. 'No use at all,' he agreed.

Karen put her lips to the broad chest, allowing her instincts full sway as she kissed her way down to where the sheet lay across his hipline, thankful to feel his response. He was right. They had to carry on with their lives the way they would have done if there had been no disruption. Children were part and parcel of a marriage.

She could only hope the doctors had been right in their assessment of future risks.

The puppy Luiz brought in a couple of days later was a bit of a mixed variety with its roly-poly body, long tail and over-sized paws, but Karen was entranced from the word go. She named the little creature Samson to compensate for his lack of stature.

Beatriz, naturally, found everything wrong with having an animal of any kind loose in the house, although she tended to keep her opinions low-key when Luiz was within hearing.

'She just looks for faults to find,' Regina declared, enraptured herself with the new addition. 'Luiz said Samson was one of a litter of five. Perhaps I could have one of the others for myself.'

That would really give Beatriz something to complain about, Karen reflected.

'Would *you* ask Luiz?' Regina added ingenuously. 'He can refuse you nothing.'

Karen doubted that. Their relationship out of bed was nowhere near as clear-cut as it was in it.

'I'll try,' she promised. 'But don't count on anything.'

His response when she did put Regina's request that night wasn't immediately encouraging. His sister had never shown any interest in animals as pets before this, he said. It would just be an impulse on her part.

'If it did turn out to be, I'd happily be responsible for both animals,' Karen declared. 'But I think you're doing her an injustice.'

'You mean she's unlikely to change her mind?' he asked on an ironic note. 'There are a number of past occasions which would give the lie to that.'

'There's a big difference between passing fancies in boyfriends and this,' Karen protested.

'You believe so?' He studied her, his expression difficult to read. 'Regina idolises you. You must realise that. Where you lead, she will follow. A responsibility in itself.'

'I love her too.' Karen could say that with truth. 'Let her have the pup, Luiz. She'll look after it, I'm certain.'

He inclined his head. 'I'll leave it to you to tell Beatriz.'

'Coward,' she taunted lightly, and saw a glint spring suddenly in his eyes.

He took a swift step forward and swung her up in his arms, carrying her across to dump her face down on the bed, holding her there with a hand between her shoulder blades. 'Apologise, or pay the price,' he threatened.

Karen held up her hands in mock surrender. 'I apologise, I apologise!'

He turned her over but didn't let her up, humour giving way to a more potent emotion as he surveyed her lovely laughing face. It would have been like this in the beginning, Karen thought yearningly, meeting his lips: so different from the trials and tribulations of the past weeks.

Lying sated but sleepless later, she wondered if a psychiatrist might help her break through the block in her memory. Or even a hypnotist.

Yet did she really want to know the truth? came the sneaking thought. Whatever it was that had sent her careering off to Rio, it was in the past, and probably best left that way.

Luiz stirred, the arm curved about her waist drawing her closer against him. The very feel of him was a stimulus. She ran her fingertips along one taut thigh, feeling the muscle tense to her touch. He opened his eyes as she found him, his response immediate.

'I believed you satisfied,' he said softly.

'That was then,' she responded, 'this is now. It's your own fault. You shouldn't make it so fantastic!'

He gave a low laugh and rolled on top of her, joining the two of them together again in one fluid movement. 'You may live to regret your boldness,' he declared.

She may live to regret a lot of things, but never this! she thought.

Predictably, two healthy, lively pups left a certain amount of havoc in their wake. The household staff took a tolerant view, Beatriz anything but. More than once it was on the tip of Karen's tongue to suggest that she and Raymundo find a home of their own if this one no longer suited, but it was Luiz's place to make that decision, not hers.

The despondency she felt on receiving proof that she wasn't pregnant went deeper than she would have anticipated. Luiz appeared philosophical about it, but she sensed his disappointment.

'Supposing it never happens again?' she said. 'Supposing I can never give you a son to take over Guavada?'

'Better the positive than the negative outlook,' he returned. Eyes veiled, he drew her to him to kiss her. 'There's no shortage of time.'

Certainly no shortage of effort, Karen reflected, wondering how he was going to cope with several celibate nights, wondering how *she* was going to cope, for that matter.

It proved no problem because Luiz wouldn't allow it to be. There were pleasure zones still to be explored, she found. If she had one wish, it would be for them both to be able to say the words that really meant something, but there were too many unanswered questions for it to be likely. How could there be love where there was no trust?

* * *

March brought slightly cooler, though still pleasant temperatures, along with a sharp decrease in rainfall.

It was exactly six weeks since she'd woken up in that hospital bed, Karen realised one morning, checking the date; some four and a half months since she'd won the money that had totally changed her life.

The major part of that time was still a great big blank. She'd accepted the probability that it always would be. She still suffered the occasional nostalgic pang at the thought of what she'd left behind in England, but she had to admit that there was no comparison between the life she had led there and what she had here.

Her only real complaint was that she saw so relatively little of Luiz during the day. Apart from the time he spent out on the ranch, he had an office right here in the house equipped with enough technological paraphernalia to keep several businesses going. Unlike Raymundo, who was happy to sit back and allow others control of his affairs, he preferred full involvement.

'Maybe I could help out in some way?' she suggested one evening. 'I'm conversant with computers, and all that.'

Luiz laughed. 'I don't doubt your intelligence, but it isn't necessary.'

'Meaning you don't want me meddling in your affairs?' she responded on a note that drew a sudden line between the dark brows.

'Meaning I prefer to work alone. You surely have enough to occupy you. Especially now that you're driving again.' He studied her, the frown deepening. 'You find your life here boring?'

'No, of course not,' she denied. 'It's just so different from what I'm used to.'

'Your old life is almost six months past and gone,' he returned.

'Not to me,' she said. 'Or had you forgotten?'

She regretted the retort the moment the words left her lips, seeing his jaw harden. 'Joke!' she added in an attempt at humour that fell miserably flat.

'A very poor one,' he remarked. '*I* can forget nothing!'

'Luiz, I'm sorry!' Karen caught his arm as he made to turn away. 'I realise how hard it is for you too. I just...'

'You needed to hit out,' he finished for her as she broke off. 'I know the feeling well.' His lips slanted at the expression that sprang in her eyes. 'Not physically. You never had anything to fear from me in that sense.'

'I know,' she said, and saw the sardonic smile come again.

'You can't *know* anything about those three months.'

'I'm sure I'd sense it if I'd ever had cause to be afraid of you.' She was desperate to undo the harm she'd done. 'The same way I'd sense having been with any other man but you!'

For a lengthy moment he didn't move, searching her face feature by feature with an intensity that pierced her. Karen reached up to kiss him on the lips, putting everything she'd learned these last weeks into persuading the firmness to soften.

'I want you!' she whispered, abandoning all other trains of thought in the swift flaring of passion.

There was no verbal reply, just an answering flame in the dark eyes. Karen clung to him as he lifted her to carry her to the bed. This wasn't the answer to everything, but right now it was enough.

The pups showed signs of outstripping all expectations with regard to ultimate size. Banned from the house when Beatriz finally won the day after the pair of them ripped up a couple of rugs, they were given a new home in the grounds, complete with outside run and a kennel equipped, at Karen's demand, with heating against the chill of the coming winter nights. Regina had to a large extent lost interest in the animals, although she did play with them on occasion.

'I won't say I told you so,' Luiz remarked on finding Karen walking the two of them on her own one afternoon.

'You just did,' she returned. 'So you were right. It's no big problem.'

'It seems it might become a very big problem,' he said, assessing the difficulty she was having in controlling the pair. 'They're too strong for you now. How will you cope when they're fully grown?'

'They'll be trained by then,' she declared with more hope than faith. 'All it takes is perseverance.'

'Yes, I can see how well they're learning to obey you.'

The mockery lit a spark in her eyes. 'We can't all be despots!'

Dark brows lifted in sardonic amusement. 'A tyrant, am I?'

She had to smile. 'All right, so it was a bit over the top. Don't give Regina a hard time though. She'll think I've been complaining about her.'

'So you should,' he said. 'She puts too much reliance on your good nature.' He indicated that she hand over the leads. 'I'll walk them back to the compound and save a little wear and tear on your arm muscles.'

Karen obeyed, not in the least surprised when both animals followed the same impulse, falling into docile step at his side.

'You're not going to suggest Bruno goes, I hope,' she said tentatively. 'Samson would be lonely without him.'

'He can stay if you agree to let Carlos take the pair of them in hand.'

'Not if he's going to beat obedience into them. I won't have them cowed!'

'I'll make sure he treats them well.' There was a pause before he spoke again, his tone subtly altered. 'I have to go to Brasilia.'

'To see your mother?'

'I'll call on her while I'm there, but I have other business to attend to.'

Karen shot him a glance, drawn by some instinct she couldn't explain. His expression gave nothing away.

'How long will you be gone?' she asked.

'Two days, perhaps three. No more than that.'

'When?'

'Tomorrow.'

She swallowed on the sudden dryness in her throat, wondering if she was coming down with something. 'I'll miss you.'

His smile was brief. 'By night at least.'

It was a moment before she could find the words. 'You think sex is all I care about?'

'I think it plays a major part in our relationship,' he answered levelly. 'And always did.'

Karen forced herself to continue walking. 'You're saying I never felt any more than that for you?'

'I believe you convinced yourself that you did. I convinced myself for a time.'

'Until the day I proved otherwise by running out on you.' Her tone was as flat as his. 'You still believe I went off with Lucio Fernandas, don't you?'

'I can find no other reason,' he admitted. 'He left that same day without telling anyone he was going.'

She shook her head emphatically. 'There's no way I could have been drawn to a man of his type!'

'Many other women were. He was renowned for his conquests.'

'You've been making enquiries about him?'

'I needed none. His reputation was well-known.'

'But you still kept him in your employ.'

'Providing he does the job he's paid to do, a man's private life is his own.'

'Unless it encroaches on yours, of course!'

The sarcasm left him unmoved. 'True. Medical opinion appears to be that partial amnesia of the kind you're suffering from is the mind's way of blocking out what it doesn't want to remember. If the blockage is permanent, the only way I can ever be sure there was nothing between the two of you is to have him tell me so himself.'

'And how do you propose doing that, when you don't know where he is?'

'I've employed someone to try and trace him.'

Karen felt more than a flicker of apprehension. It was all very well to tell herself she wouldn't have gone near a man of the kind Lucio Fernandas appeared to be, but how could she be certain? How could she be certain of *anything*?

'I hope they succeed,' she said, knowing it was only a half-truth.

Luiz left the subject alone after that, but it was obvious that it was never going to stop preying on his mind. It had begun preying on her own again. Lucio Fernandas had been on the same flight on the same day after walking out on his job without a word to anyone. What other explanation was there?

They had people coming to dinner that evening. Nothing too formal, just a gathering of friends. Karen chose a slub silk skirt and sleeveless top, sliding her feet into high-heeled sandals. With the pups to exercise several times a day, she'd become accustomed to wearing flats. It felt good to stand tall again.

Her prowess in the language made socialising a great deal easier. If anyone felt any awkwardness over her amnesia these days, they hid it well.

Even Beatriz made some effort to conceal her feelings in company. Watching her surreptitiously as she conversed with the man seated next to her, Karen thought how different she looked when she smiled. There was no chance, she knew, of them ever becoming friends. She had the man Beatriz had really wanted. Nothing was going to change that.

Raymundo might appear to be oblivious of his wife's preference, but he couldn't be totally unaware. She often felt like telling him to stand up for himself when Beatriz was in one of her moods and finding fault with everything he said or did, but she held it back. Luiz had simply shrugged when she brought the subject up, and said it was up to Raymundo to command some respect. Beatriz certainly took no liberties with him.

Seated at the head of the table, the pure white silk of his shirt a foil for the olive skin of his face and throat, he made her ache. He was so wrong when he said sex was the driving force in their relationship. A vital force, yes, but there was so much more to the emotions he aroused in her now.

If she'd felt as deeply as this for him before, wild horses couldn't have dragged her away from him, she was sure. So what had made the difference?

With the night-time temperature a little too cool now for coffee out on the veranda, the party adjourned to one of the spacious living rooms. Conversation went on apace. Karen did her best to keep up, but her mind wasn't really on it. She didn't even know what time Luiz was planning on leaving tomorrow, she realised.

Regina came to sit beside her, her lovely young face lit by an inner glow.

'So what do you think of him?' she asked eagerly.

Karen brought her thoughts back to the here and now, wrinkling her brow in query. 'Think of whom?'

'Miran, of course. Miran Villota!'

Karen turned her attention to the young man in question. Miran was in his mid-twenties and extremely good-looking, with a dashing air about him scheduled to appeal to any girl. He was visiting the Ferrez's, hence his inclusion in tonight's invitation.

'He seems nice enough,' she pronounced.

'Nice!' Regina looked affronted. 'Is that all you can say?'

Karen kept her face straight with an effort. 'What else would you like me to say? I've only spoken with him a couple of times. Hardly enough to make an evaluation.'

'*I* find him excellent in every way,' Regina claimed. 'He lives and works in São Paulo, but he travels a great deal too. He knows so much of the world!'

'Is that what you'd like yourself?' Karen asked. 'To travel, I mean?'

'Of course. There are many places I want to see. I could do that with Miran.'

Karen held up a staying hand. 'Whoa a minute! You only just met him!'

'You told me you knew the moment you saw Luiz that he was the one,' came the rejoinder. 'I feel the same way about Miran.'

Nonplussed, Karen said cautiously, 'But does he feel the same way about you?'

The dark eyes glowed. 'He tells me so.'

'When did he do that?'

'When we were together at the table. He said I'm the most beautiful girl he's ever seen. He said he has never felt such an instant rapport before with anyone!'

Karen hardly knew what to answer. She'd noticed the two of them talking together once or twice, but had been too involved in the conversations going on around her to pay much attention.

'All the same, it's a bit soon to be thinking along the lines you're thinking,' she ventured.

'Why?' Regina demanded. 'It happened for you and Luiz, why not for Miran and me? I was never so certain of anything as I am of this!'

'You were certain you wanted a puppy not so long ago,' Karen pointed out, instantly regretting the remark. 'Sorry, that was unfair,' she apologised.

'Yes, it was.' Regina's chin was up, her eyes sparkling. 'Miran is not to be compared with a pet animal!'

'Of course not.' Karen hesitated, still not sure how

best to tackle the situation. 'I believe he'll be here for several days?'

'Four more days,' Regina confirmed. 'We're to meet tomorrow in La Santa for lunch together.'

It was hardly fair to dismiss her sister-in-law's feelings for Miran Villota out of hand, Karen decided. His either, for that matter. As a friend of the Ferrez family, he surely had to be trustworthy.

'I'll look forward to hearing more tomorrow then,' she said.

It was almost two in the morning before everyone left. Karen saw Regina and Miran exchanging meaningful glances on his departure, although there was no physical contact between them.

'I think it a good thing Miran will only be here for a few days,' Luiz commented as they prepared for bed, proving he hadn't been blind to the exchange either. 'He's no unseasoned youth.'

'He can't be all that much older than I am,' Karen murmured.

'In years, perhaps. In experience…' He left the sentence unfinished, his tone enough.

Definitely *not* the time to tell him what Regina had in mind, Karen reflected wryly. He might have gone overboard himself at one time, but he was unlikely to view Regina's captivation in the same light.

'Men tend to be, don't they?' she said, trying for a humorous tone. 'More experienced, I mean. You certainly were.'

He gave her an ironic glance. 'How can you be sure of that?'

She laughed. 'You wouldn't try claiming I was the first for you too?'

'Perhaps not. But I was always selective.'

'Perhaps Miran Villota has been too,' she said.

Luiz studied her thoughtfully. 'Why do you feel it necessary to defend him?'

'I'm just suggesting that you could be wrong about him, that's all.'

'An opinion based on a few minutes conversation?'

'I'm going on instinct,' she claimed. 'Feminine instinct.'

'Not always dependable.'

'What time will you be leaving in the morning?' Karen asked, wishing she'd kept her mouth shut.

It was obvious from his expression that he found the change of subject questionable, but he responded. 'My flight is at noon. I must leave here no later than eight-thirty.'

It was half past two now, which gave them a good five hours before they need get up, Karen calculated. She thrust all other thoughts aside as she slid into the bed alongside him, heart racing as always in anticipation when he turned to her. Little more than a brushing of his lips, the kiss left her high and dry.

He was asleep within moments, to judge from his breathing. Lying there in the darkness, Karen took herself to task for feeling deprived. So it was the first time he'd failed to make love to her in one way or another. There had to be a first time. With a lengthy drive to the airport ahead of him, he needed to be alert.

There was more to it than that, she knew. He hadn't liked her seeming defence of Miran. She'd been doing it for Regina's sake, but he wasn't to know that. In his eyes, the interest was hers.

She considered waking him to tell him it was nonsense, but it was probably best to let the whole thing lie. By the time he returned, Regina would hopefully have come to her senses, and Miran Villota could be forgotten by all.

It was a long time before she slept, and already well gone nine when she awoke. There wasn't much point rushing around in the hope that Luiz hadn't yet left, she acknowledged disconsolately. The house already felt empty.

Regina greeted her eagerly when she finally went down. She was still over the moon with regard to Miran, still convinced that she had found the love of her life.

'Today I tell him what I feel for him,' she declared happily.

Karen wondered just what his reaction would be. Everything Regina had told her he had said to her last night was no more than any man might say to any woman he was attracted to. Any Latin, at any rate. Yes, he'd asked to see her today, but it didn't add up to all that much. So far, they hadn't even kissed!

Regina was still starry-eyed when she returned from the lunch date, although a little disappointed that Miran had declined her invitation to come back with her. He had business to take care of, she said. They hadn't actually discussed the future yet. They'd had so much else to talk about.

'He is so wonderful!' She sighed. 'I told him how you and Luiz knew instantly that you were meant for each other too.'

'What did he say to that?' asked Karen tentatively.

'He thought it very romantic. As it was, of course. As it is now for the two of us!'

'So when are you seeing him again?'

'He is to telephone me to make the arrangement.'

Hardly the action of a man reluctant to be parted

from his loved one for longer than absolutely necessary, Karen reflected, though who was she to judge?

'You realise Luiz is unlikely to approve?' she said.

'Luiz can't stop me marrying Miran,' came the undaunted response.

He'd certainly have a darn good try, Karen thought. Not that she was convinced it was any of it more than pie in the sky as yet. The only way to find out what Miran's feelings really were was to ask him outright, and at the earliest opportunity.

How to get in touch was the problem. She could telephone the Ferrez home and ask to speak to him, but considering Luiz's attitude last night, and the possibility of his discovering she had made the call, that might not be a good idea. Lucio Fernandas still loomed too large in their lives.

The problem was resolved when she was called to the phone herself that evening. Expecting it to be Luiz on the line, she was nonplussed when the call turned out to be from Miran.

'I have to talk with you,' he said urgently. 'About Regina?' Karen asked.

'About Regina, yes,' he said. 'I can't discuss the matter now. Someone might hear. Will you meet with me?'

She hesitated, already suspecting the truth. 'You should speak with Regina herself.'

'I can't do that. Please! I beg of you!'

Short of refusing point-blank, she was left with little choice, Karen accepted resignedly. She should have told Luiz what was going on last night and let him sort it all out.

'All right,' she said. 'Where and when?'

'I have commitments in the morning, and for lunch,

but I'll be free by half past three. I'll wait at the market square. I must go now,' he added before she could answer.

Karen replaced the receiver feeling anything but happy with the arrangement. There was no market in town tomorrow, but there would still be plenty of people around the square. She was pretty sure what Miran was going to say. Regina had gained entirely the wrong impression, and he didn't know how to tell her.

Which meant she was probably going to get the job.

'Was that Luiz?' Beatriz asked.

Karen forced herself to turn without haste to view the woman standing a few yards away. 'Yes,' she said, realising she would have a hard time explaining if Luiz happened to ring while they were standing here. 'He had a good journey,' she added lamely.

Beatriz curled a lip. 'That is all he had to say to you?'

'No.' Karen was hard put to it to keep a civil tongue in her head. 'The rest is between husband and wife.'

'You can hide from the truth, but you can't escape it for ever!' Beatriz spat after her as she started to turn away.

It was something in her tone as much as the words themselves that pulled Karen up. The shaft of pain lancing her head was reminiscent of that day back on Corcovado when she'd first heard Beatriz's name mentioned. She swallowed thickly on the sudden blockage in her throat.

'What are you talking about?' she managed to get out.

The malice in the amber eyes was soul-searing. 'You think the business Luiz has in Brasilia concerns

Guavada. If you wish to remind yourself of what it does concern, you'll find the proof in his office desk.'

Karen stood rooted to the spot for several moments after Beatriz left her. Her head was gripped by a vice, her mind spinning in endless circles out of which no coherent thought emerged. When she did eventually move it was like an automaton obeying a programmed instruction.

She had only been in the office a couple of times these past weeks. Standing in the doorway, she surveyed the room with eyes blanked of all expression.

The big dark wood desk was by the window, flanked by others bearing various pieces of equipment. She crossed to it, ignoring the papers spread across the surface to start rifling through the drawers.

She found what she wasn't even sure she was looking for in one of the bottom ones. Face ravishingly lovely beneath gleaming coils of black hair, the girl portrayed was no more than eighteen. She held a child on her lap: a boy of perhaps two years old, his dark curly hair and emerging features only too recognisable.

The photograph gripped in her hand, Karen sank nervelessly into the chair as the fog finally lifted…

CHAPTER SEVEN

TALL and lean, shoulders broad beneath the close fitting white T-shirt, he drew every female eye in the vicinity. Karen was no exception. The lurch in the pit of her stomach as she took in the planes and angles of his face beneath the pelt of curly black hair needed no explanation. There was no shortage of good-looking macho males in Rio, but he was the first to have this effect on her on mere sight.

He paused in the restaurant doorway, surveying the crowded room without haste. Karen shifted her gaze back to her plate as his eyes came to rest on her, feeling the increase in her pulse rate. In a country where most women were dark-haired, her colouring alone made her stand out. She'd been subjected to several unwelcome approaches since she'd arrived in Rio. The price to be paid by a woman travelling alone.

Her stomach muscles jerked again as the *maître d'* appeared at her elbow.

'We have a problem, *senhorita*,' he said deferentially. 'This is the only table with a seat not taken. Would you allow Senhor Andrade the use of it?'

Karen didn't need to look beyond him to know who Senhor Andrade was. She could sense his presence. There was only one response she could make without appearing churlish—and churlishness was farthest from her mind right now.

'Of course,' she said.

The smile her new companion gave her as he slid

into the chair directly opposite was devastating. She could only hope her expression was as unrevealing as she tried to make it.

'This is very accommodating of you,' he said in excellent though heavily accented English. 'You're here on vacation?'

'Holiday,' she corrected lightly. 'In England we say holiday. And yes, I am.'

'Alone?'

Her chin tilted, green eyes acquiring a faint spark. 'Yes.'

'Rio is no place for a woman like you to visit alone,' he declared. 'Your hair alone is a beacon.'

'Maybe I should consider dyeing it,' she said with deliberate flippancy.

'That would be a crime in itself.'

He took the menu from the waiter who had just appeared and ran his eyes down it, reeled off the name of a dish and handed it back with a request for the wine waiter to attend.

'You will join me in a glass of wine?' he asked.

Be a bit of a tight fit, it was on the tip of her tongue to retort; she bit it back because humour of such an infantile kind was unlikely to be appreciated.

'Thank you, but I'm quite happy with the water,' she said, with a sudden notion that she was going to need to keep a steady head.

Dark as night, his regard gave her palpitations. She wanted to look away, but she couldn't, mesmerised by the tiny amber sparks deep down in the blackness.

'My name is Luiz,' he said. 'The management will vouch for me if you find it necessary.'

'Why might I find it necessary?' she asked, and saw

the firmly moulded mouth take on a curve that set her pulses racing all over again.

'Why indeed?' The pause was brief. 'You still have to tell me your name.'

'It's Karen Downing.'

'Karen.' His voice caressed the word. 'You're very beautiful. Too much so to be alone by anything but choice. Is there no man in your life?'

Not until now, came the unbidden thought.

'I'm footloose and fancy free,' she quipped, trying to keep a grip on herself. 'To travel alone is to travel fastest!'

'Have you been long in Brazil?'

'Just three days. I've wanted to visit Rio ever since I first saw it in a travelogue.'

'And does it meet with your expectations?'

'The scenery certainly does. I went up Sugar Loaf yesterday. The view is tremendous!'

'The view from Corcovado is even more spectacular,' he said. 'I'll drive you up there this afternoon through the rainforest.'

Karen gazed at him with lifted brows, fighting the mad inclination to just go along with anything he suggested. 'You're taking rather a lot for granted.'

'No more than my senses tell me should be taken.' The tone was soft, his gaze spellbinding. 'You'd deny the attraction between us?'

'We only just met,' she protested faintly.

'But we were destined to meet,' he said. 'I've waited many years for this moment—this certainty. You feel it too.'

Right now, Karen wasn't sure *what* she felt. Her head was spinning. He was right about the attraction—

her every sense was fired by it—but giving way to it was another matter.

'I really don't think—' she began.

'Then don't think,' he cut in. 'Just follow what your heart tells you. You want what I want. *Everything* I want! I see it in your eyes.'

Coming from any other man, she would have called that the most supreme egotism, but what he said was too close to the truth to be dismissed that way. She'd been attracted to men on occasion, but never physically aroused as she was right now. Her skin felt as if ants were crawling over it, her insides turned fluid.

Go with it, an inner voice urged. Live dangerously for once!

She gave a slightly shaky laugh. 'As a line, I have to admit it's a good one!'

'I speak no line. Only what I feel. You stir me the way no other woman ever stirred me.'

'Why?' she queried helplessly.

'Your beauty alone could be reason enough, but I sense a great deal more to you than that. Fate brought you here to Rio for a purpose.'

'A lottery win brought me here,' she said on as pragmatic a note as she could manage. 'I could never have afforded it otherwise. It will almost all be gone by the time I get home, so if it's money you're after…'

She broke off as amusement danced in his eyes. 'You think I appear in need of money?' he asked.

'No,' she admitted. 'I just thought I should make it clear.'

'I take due note.' Amusement still gleamed. 'The allure is more than sufficient as it stands, I assure you.'

Gazing at him, Karen knew a sudden devil-may-care surge. Luiz Andrade was like no other man she had ever met—like none she was ever likely to meet again. Practised in the art of seduction for certain, yet she somehow trusted him.

'Shall I need to change?' she asked. 'For the drive, I mean.'

Viewing the sleeveless lemon top outlining firm breasts, he shook his head. 'You're perfect just as you are.'

Karen had enjoyed seeing Rio on her own, but not nearly as much as with Luiz for a guide. She found herself telling him just about her whole life story, and hearing many details of his.

After completing the business that had brought him to Rio, he had decided to take a few days to himself before returning home, moving into the hotel that very morning. A man of some means, she gathered, reading between the lines. Wealthy enough to have little need of finding a rich woman to fleece, for certain.

'You must have thought me very gauche to come out with an accusation like that,' she said ruefully at one point.

'I found your lack of conceit in suspecting money might have a bearing on my interest utterly delightful,' Luiz returned. 'You have no real concept of the effect you have on a man, have you?' he added.

They were alone on the highest of the Corcovado platforms, immediately beneath the towering figure of Christ. Karen felt her throat dry as he slid a hand beneath her hair to tilt her face to his.

The kiss was gentle at first, almost playful, lips brushing, nibbling, teasing hers apart. She was lost to everything but the feel of him, the masculine scent of him, the warmth spiralling through her body.

The silky touch of his tongue sent a shudder rippling down her back, inciting a response she couldn't, and didn't want to, control. She slid her arms about his shoulders, fingers seeking the curl of hair at his nape. Somewhere in the back of her mind she regretted her lack of high heels to bring the lower half of her body into closer contact with his: a need fulfilled when he drew her up to him.

He was aroused himself, but still in control, the proof of that in his failure to take further advantage of her inflamed emotions. Karen came back to earth with a thud as he put her firmly from him.

'Tonight we dance together,' he murmured.

'You're taking a lot for granted again,' she got out.

A wicked sparkle lit the dark eyes. 'I speak of the Samba. In Rio, everyone dances the Samba!'

Karen had to smile. The Samba might come first, but she knew where the day was going to end—knew where she wanted it to end. What happened after that she couldn't find the will to care.

It was already approaching eight o'clock when they returned to the hotel. Back in her luxurious room, she took a shower and donned a simple blue sheath of a dress for the evening, adorning it with the single strand of small cultured pearls that had been her mother's.

Falling from a central parting, her hair framed the pure oval of a face too familiar to her to be viewed with any overriding vanity. It appealed to Luiz. That was all that mattered. She only hoped she didn't disappoint him too much in other ways when the time came.

They ate dinner in one of the hotel restaurants, continuing on from there to a private club. Devastating in a white tuxedo, Luiz guided her through a whole selection of Latin American dances, creating havoc with a tango that had her moulded to his body like a second skin.

'If they could see me now!' she quipped breathlessly when the music stopped.

'If who could see you now?' Luiz asked, still holding her close.

'Friends back home. They'll never believe I did that!' She gave a laugh, eyes sparkling up at him. 'I can hardly believe it myself! It was so…'

'Sensual?' he supplied as she searched for the right word. 'It's meant to be. The prelude to lovemaking.' His voice was low, his gaze intent on her face, his expression leaving nothing to doubt. 'I want to make love to you. I ache for it!'

'Me too,' she whispered, abandoning what little emotional control she had left.

He kissed her then, ignoring the others on the floor. Karen returned it without reserve. She knew no embarrassment on feeling knowing eyes on them as he led her from the floor. So what if people did guess where they were heading? It happened the world over.

It was almost one o'clock when they reached the hotel. By silent consent they went to her room. Karen knew a momentary misgiving as Luiz quietly closed the door, but it vanished as he took her in his arms to kiss her with overriding passion.

He undressed her with dexterity, caressing each freshly exposed portion of her body. Her breasts filled his palms, nipples small and pink. She cried out at the exquisite sensation when he took them between his lips.

Stripped himself, he was everything she had imagined: skin taut over smoothly honed muscle, chest lightly covered in curling black hair, hips lean and hard, the proud manhood shortening her breath. She wished desperately that she was experienced in love-making, knowledgeable in the sexual arts.

'Is it possible that this is your first time with a man?' he asked softly, sensing the constraint in her.

'Yes,' she confessed. 'I'm sorry to disappoint you.'

'Disappoint me!' He added something in his own language, eyes charged with those sparkling amber lights. 'That you could never do. Surrender yourself to me! Let me show you the way!'

From that moment time dissolved. All she knew was sensation after rippling sensation as Luiz introduced her to erogenous zones she hadn't even known her body possessed. Reticence withered and died beneath the skilful caresses, a sensuality she had never dared acknowledge before prompting her to answer in kind. Exploring him as he was exploring her, to fetch the breath hissing through his teeth and glory in the power.

When the moment came, she was so aroused she felt barely any pain at all as he carved a passage to the molten centre of her body. The feel of him inside her went beyond anything she had ever imagined, filling her, claiming her. She almost passed out at the peak, body arching as spasm after spasm shook her.

Supporting himself on bent elbows, Luiz looked down into her drowned face with gratification.

'You belong to me now,' he said. 'For all time! I'll allow no other man to know you. We'll be married as soon as it can be arranged.' He smiled as her eyes flew open in shock. 'You must know what I feel for you. What you feel for me. There can be no other way.'

'I'm only here for two weeks,' she whispered, unable to believe he really meant it. 'My home is in England.'

'You have no family to draw you back there.'

'I have friends.'

'And they mean more to you than what exists between us?'

'This is just...physical,' she got out. 'I'm sure you've felt the same way over other women.'

Dark eyes blazed in repudiation. 'Never! Neither can you have ever felt this way for another man, or you would have already given yourself.'

He put his lips to hers again, robbing her of the ability to think straight—even to think at all. His tongue slid silkily into the softness, making her quiver as passion rose in her once more.

'You see,' he murmured when the world had stopped spinning again. 'We belong together. Can you deny the strength of our feelings?'

Karen couldn't, and had no desire to. What kind of fool would she be, she asked herself, to turn her back on the only man she'd ever met who could make her feel this way? A man who wanted far more than just her body. What did she really have back home to return to? Friends might miss her for a while, but they had lives of their own to get on with.

Luiz read the response in her eyes, his own registering a depth of emotion that shook her to the core. She drew him down to her to kiss him with tremulous intensity, closing out the reservations nibbling at the corners of her mind.

There were moments during the days following when those reservations surfaced again, but one look at Luiz was enough to push them back under. He was so much the macho male. She felt protected, cared about—all the things she'd missed so much these past four years since her parents had gone.

The phone call home to tell her flatmate she wouldn't be returning was received with initial disbelief. How could she possibly marry a man she'd known such a short time, and a foreigner at that? Julie demanded. What about her job, her belongings, her whole life?

Apart from certain mementos, nothing was important compared with Luiz, Karen told her, refusing to acknowledge even the faintest doubt.

If Luiz entertained any doubts of his own, he gave no sign of it. They spent the days doing all the things Karen had planned to do: visiting the sights, lounging on the famous beaches, swimming in the warm blue sea. At night they made love, each time better than the last. For Karen it was a dream world where nothing could intrude. She floated on air.

The wedding, a civil ceremony, took place just a week after her arrival in Rio. There would be a church blessing when they were home in São Paulo, Luiz had promised.

He wanted it this way, he said when she asked why they didn't wait until they got to São Paulo to get married, which made her suspect him of presenting a probably disapproving family with a *fait accompli*. Not that she allowed the suspicion to affect her. She was marrying the man, not the family.

Only on completing the formalities did it strike home that she'd really and truly burned her boats. Karen Downing was no more. In her place stood

Senhora Andrade, wife of a man still a stranger in many ways.

'Do your brother and sister know about the wedding yet?' she asked that night after their tumultuous love-making.

'They do,' Luiz confirmed.

'But they didn't want to be here for it?'

'Regina wanted to come,' he admitted, 'but I forbade her to travel alone.'

'And your brother?' she said after a moment.

There was a brief pause before he answered, his tone dispassionate. 'Raymundo allows himself to be ruled by his wife's opinions.'

Karen kept her tone light. 'Something you'd never do!'

'Ruled, no,' he agreed. 'Beatriz might form some respect for her husband if he began making his own decisions.'

'I take it, then, that your sister-in-law is the fly in the ointment,' she said.

His laugh was dry. 'If that means she is the one least likely to offer you a welcome, then yes. Not that you must allow her to undermine your position. You will be head of the household.'

'Under you, of course,' she murmured in mock humility.

He rolled on to his back to pull her on top of him, eyes glinting up at her as he fitted her to him. 'Not always,' he said.

Karen gave herself over to the exquisite sensations, loving his mastery. No regrets, was her last fading thought.

She would have preferred a little more time with

Luiz on his own, but he didn't give her the option. They travelled to São Paulo the following day.

After the heat and humidity of Rio, the drier, milder climate of the São Paulo plateau was a wonderful relief.

'Happy?' Luiz asked as they drove away from the airport in the car he'd left there on his departure.

'Blissfully!' she said. She hesitated before adding, 'I'll be even happier once I've got the meeting with your family over.'

'They'll love you,' he declared. The glance he turned her way was heart-warming. 'They can do no other!'

'You're biased,' she teased.

Luiz looked her way again, eyes skimming her glowing, sun-bronzed face, the silver fall of her hair, the smooth line of her throat revealed by the open collar of her cream silk shirt.

'I adore you,' he said. 'Every inch of you!' The wicked sparkle danced in his eyes. 'And I *know* every inch of you!'

She could verify that, Karen thought, senses fired by the mere memory of last night's excesses. She had believed they'd already reached the pinnacle, but he'd proved her wrong. She watched his hands on the wheel, lean and long fingered, the nails trimmed short and smoothly filed, wrists supple. Those hands alone had afforded her more pleasure than she had ever thought possible.

Tonight they would share a bed again, but first she had to contend with meeting her new relatives. From what Luiz had said, his sister-in-law was the only one unlikely to extend a welcome, but the marriage would have been a shock for them all. She could hardly blame Regina and Raymundo if they held back too.

Expecting more of a village than a town, she found La Santa enough of a surprise, but the house and landscaped grounds took her breath away. Knowing Luiz was no pauper was one thing, realising that the ranch probably formed only a part of his assets quite another. She was married to a man of means way beyond her imaginings.

Regina greeted her with open arms, her lovely young face lit with pleasure and excitement.

'Luiz said you were beautiful,' she exclaimed, 'but never have I seen hair the colour of yours before!'

'Inherited from my mother,' Karen told her, warmed beyond measure by the reception. 'I always wanted a sister. Now I have one!'

'And a brother,' said Raymundo, coming forward to kiss her on both cheeks. 'Welcome to Guavada!'

He seemed genuine too, Karen thought, smiling back at him. Odd that someone who looked so much like Luiz could leave her totally unstirred.

The woman at his back made no attempt to offer an embrace. Her striking features were expressionless.

She said something in Portuguese, drawing a frown from Luiz.

'Karen has no knowledge of the language yet,' he said. 'We'll all of us speak English alone in her company for the present.'

'I want to learn the language,' Karen protested.

'Which you will,' he said. 'In time.' His smile was for her and her alone. 'We have a lifetime ahead of us.'

A lifetime in a country she knew next to nothing about, with a man she knew little more about, came the thought, pushed hastily to the back of her mind where it could do least harm.

Her spirits lifted again in the privacy of the bedroom when Luiz took her in his arms to welcome her home his own way. *This* was what counted the most, she told herself.

She clung to that thought during those first days. Adjusting to a lifestyle totally different from what she was accustomed to proved far from easy. She suffered badly from homesickness at times.

With a manager to oversee the day-to-day running of the ranch, Luiz hardly needed to be involved in any physical sense himself, but he was often out riding the range with the men—even turning his hand to manual labour on occasion.

'I enjoy it,' he said simply when Karen questioned the necessity. 'It fulfils me. A different kind of fulfilment,' he added, seeing the expression in her eyes. 'Not to be compared.'

'I should hope not,' she said, doing her best to be rational about it.

He laughed, gathering her to him to kiss her with undiminished ardour. 'As if anything could possibly compare with the pleasure you give me!'

Maybe not in the same way, came the thought, but she was still only a part of his life.

He had been the focus of hers back in Rio, blinding her to everything else. Here at Guavada, she was beginning to realise the enormity of the step she had taken. Abandoning the country of her birth to live a life totally alien to her with a man she barely knew had been utterly crazy.

Not that the emotions he aroused in her were any

less intense. He only had to turn those glittering dark eyes on her to have her on fire. In his arms it was easy to convince herself that just being with him made everything worthwhile. As a lover, he was all she could ever have wished for.

A draw though his masculine assertiveness had proved in the beginning, and still was to a degree, there were times when she found it just a little overpowering too. Accepting his offer to teach her to drive instead of opting for proper lessons proved a less than sensible move.

'I read somewhere that driving lessons can spell death to a marriage,' she remarked on one occasion, trying to inject a little humour into a particularly heated exchange.

'Call me what you just called me one more time, and it's certainly death to this!' Luiz threatened, obviously not in the least amused. 'I'm not one of your English wimps!'

And I'm not one of your Brazilian doormats, it was on the tip of her tongue to retort. She bit it back because she'd not only yet to meet a woman here who could be termed a doormat in any sense, but had to admit that he had some cause for complaint over the invective she'd used just now.

'I just lost my temper for a moment,' she said placatingly.

'Then you had better learn to keep it,' he responded, the anger still glittering in his eyes.

Humour came to her rescue again, lowering her eyes in mock humility. 'I beg forgiveness,' she said.

There was no immediate response. She peeped at him from beneath her lashes, to see his mouth take on a somewhat unwilling curve.

'You,' he said, 'have no respect. I must teach you some.'

They were parked in the centre of town, with people thronging the pavements either side. Karen widened her eyes at him. 'Here?'

'Later,' he promised, unable to sustain his displeasure in the face of the emerald sparkle. 'We'll continue with *this* lesson for now.'

Lesson number one in handling her Brazilian, Karen reflected drily, putting the car into motion again: always make allowances for dented male pride, even if it did go against the grain.

Her relationship with Regina progressed by leaps and bounds. At seventeen, her sister-in-law was a romantic who found her brother's marriage in total accord with the novels she read so avidly. The heroes and heroines always finished up living happily ever after, Karen gleaned. She hoped that could be true of her and Luiz too eventually.

Attempts to get through the barriers Beatriz had erected against her met with little success. The woman treated her with open contempt when Luiz wasn't around.

'Does Raymundo have no assets of his own?' she asked Regina once.

'Of course he does,' the girl responded. 'He was left well provided for. He loves Guavada too much to make his home elsewhere.' She slanted a glance. 'Luiz would make him go if you asked it.'

'I wouldn't dream of it,' Karen denied.

'Not even to have Beatriz gone too?'

Karen gave a wry smile. 'A temptation, I admit. Why does she hate me so much?'

'Can you not guess? She would have liked to marry

Luiz herself. She took advantage of Raymundo's feelings for her to secure at least the name. Deep down, he has to know it, but she still has him in her grip.'

If that was true, and not just the product of Regina's fertile imagination, it would certainly explain a lot, Karen reflected. If it *was* true, she could feel some sympathy for Raymundo. He might be weak, but he deserved better than to be used.

With that in mind, she went out of her way to be nice to him. Away from Beatriz, he was a different person, with a sense of humour Karen delighted in drawing out.

'You and Beatriz don't really seem to have all that much in common,' she commented lightly one time when the two of them were on their own.

'No,' he agreed on a wry note. 'I can never be everything Beatriz desires.'

'You're happy to accept that?' Karen queried tentatively after a moment.

'I have no choice,' he said. 'Luiz would never sanction divorce.'

It isn't up to Luiz, Karen wanted to say, but she held it back. 'You must have loved her when you married her,' she ventured.

'I was possessed by my craving,' he admitted. 'I knew even then that it was Luiz she really wanted, but I believed I could satisfy her. It...' He broke off, expression rueful. 'I shouldn't be saying such things to you.'

'You obviously need to let it out to someone,' she said. 'Does Luiz know how you feel?'

'No.' Raymundo looked alarmed. 'You must say nothing to him!'

'I won't,' she assured him. 'But you should.'

'To what purpose?' he asked. 'I know what his answer would be.'

'That you've made your bed and must lie on it?'

A faint smile flickered at the corners of her brother-in-law's lips. 'Perhaps not in quite the same words, but the message would be the same.'

'It's *your* life, not his!' Karen was incensed. 'He has no right to tell you what you can or can't do!'

'He has the right to insist that I leave Guavada,' came the reply. 'And that I would hate.'

He closed up after that, obviously regretting having confided in her to such a degree. Karen felt both sorry for and impatient with him. Luiz may be a bit of an autocrat in some respects, but she doubted if he'd react the way Raymundo feared, regardless of his views.

Although La Santa wasn't lacking in entertainment, their social life tended to be centred more around friends and neighbours. While most appeared friendly enough on the surface, it was apparent that the marriage was looked upon with disfavour by some. Not everyone in the area spoke English, which didn't help. With her grasp of Portuguese still in its infancy, Karen was only too happy to find someone other than the Andrades themselves to converse with at one of the frequent gatherings.

Jorge Arroyo was a man of independent means, from what she could gather. He had a studio in La Santa where he dabbled in the arts, to put it in his own words. Some two or three years younger than Luiz, he had an appealingly free and easy attitude to life.

'Luiz's return with a bride ruined many hopes,' he said. 'He could have taken his choice from those still unwed. Not that any could have matched you. I yearn to capture you myself! On canvas, of course,' he added with a devilish sparkle in his eyes.

'Of course,' Karen echoed, smiling herself. 'What does one of your portraits cost?'

'There would be no sale,' he said. 'I would keep it for my eyes alone.'

'I don't somehow think Luiz would go along with that,' she responded, still in the same light vein.

He gave a mock sigh. 'I think you may be right. Luiz has little appreciation of my talents. He won't like it that you speak with me.'

Green eyes acquired a sudden spark. 'It's up to me to decide who I talk to!'

'Then I look forward to many other conversations,' he said.

He was stirring it, she thought, catching the devilish look in his eyes again as he turned away to answer some question put to him by one of the other men. Whatever his reason, she shouldn't have allowed him to provoke her.

Luiz was with a group of people a short distance away. She went to join him, slipping her hand into his, and aiming a general smile at the others. They would have been conversing in Portuguese of course, she realised, as the pause stretched.

'Do carry on,' she invited, determined not to show any discomposure. 'It's the only way I'm going to learn the language.'

'It would help you to take proper tuition,' said one of the women, not unkindly.

'I suppose it would,' Karen agreed. 'What do you think, Luiz?'

'It could do no harm,' he returned.

Karen looked at him swiftly, registering a certain

terseness in his voice. It was possible that Jorge was right, she thought, noting the tension in his jaw: he'd seen her talking with the man, and hadn't liked it. If so, it was unfortunate. She might regret what she'd said to Jorge, but she stood by the sentiment.

Luiz waited until they were home and in the privacy of the bedroom before confirming her guess. 'You'll avoid any further association with Jorge Arroyo,' he said flatly the moment the door was closed.

Half prepared though she was, Karen bristled instinctively at the tone. 'Why?' she demanded.

'It should be enough that I say so.'

'Well, I'm afraid it isn't. All I was doing was talking with the man!'

The glance he gave her was lacking its usual warmth. 'You were not just talking with him, you were flirting with him.'

'*He* was flirting,' she retorted.

'With your encouragement.' Luiz held up a hand as she made to speak. 'I want no debate.'

'Don't treat me like some second rate citizen!' she flung back. 'Where I come from, we have equality!'

He lifted a sardonic eyebrow. 'Where you come from, men have given up their right to be called men. I expect my wife to do as I ask.'

'You're not asking me,' she shot back, 'you're *telling* me!'

'So, I'm telling you.' He hadn't even raised his voice. 'You're to stay away from Jorge Arroyo.'

He turned away to head for the bathroom, leaving her seething.

She was in bed with her back turned to the centre when he returned to the room. He always slept in the nude, and she'd learned to do so too. Donning a nightdress was a gesture meant to convey her rejection.

He slid into the bed behind her without speaking. Furious though she still was, mind had little control over matter she found as his hand slid around her to seek her breast.

'Leave me alone!' she said between her teeth. 'I don't want you!'

If he'd been angry with her a few minutes ago, it obviously no longer reckoned with him. The featherlight pressure of his lips down her spine made her tingle.

'I think you lie to me,' he said softly.

She attempted to stay the movement down the length of her body to the hem of the nightdress, but he simply laughed and continued, sliding up beneath the material to find the moist centre of her being.

'Other men may desire you, but no other will ever know you this way,' he declared. 'You belong to me, and only to me!'

Body on fire, she could summon no further resistance when he drew her around to remove the gown. His lips were passionate, driving every extraneous thought from mind.

It was only afterwards, lying sleepless in his arms, that she gave way to the little voice that had been nibbling at the corners of her mind for some time. Luiz didn't love her. Not the way she'd imagined he did. She was just another possession.

CHAPTER EIGHT

ATTENDED by family and close friends, the blessing of the marriage took place at the town's magnificent church. The civil ceremony had been binding in the legal sense, but this one tied an even tighter knot. Not that she had anything to complain about, Karen acknowledged. With a wonderful home, no financial worries, and a sex-life most women would give their right arm for, she could be said to be in clover.

Confirmation of her pregnancy brought mixed emotions. It had been odds on that it would happen, of course, as no steps had been taken to stop it, but she somehow hadn't given it a thought up to now.

Luiz greeted the news with gratification. 'This won't be our only child!' he declared.

'I wouldn't want it to be.' Karen made an effort to sound as uplifted as he so obviously was. 'If this one is a boy, I'd hope the next one would be a girl.'

He laughed and shook his head. 'Two sons first. *Then* you may have a daughter.'

'I realise you're pretty strong-minded,' she returned with a slight edge, 'but some things even you can't govern!'

Luiz smiled the slow intimate smile that never failed to stir her. 'I can but try.'

Regina was delighted about the baby too, though also a little despondent.

'I think I'm destined never to meet a man I can love!' she declared soulfully.

'You're only seventeen,' Karen returned. 'You've plenty of time. Someone will come along one day and sweep you off your feet!'

'The way Luiz did with you! How did you know he was the one?' the younger girl insisted. 'What made him different from other men?'

Karen sought a light response. 'He's Brazilian.'

Her sister-in-law pulled a face. 'Now you joke with me!'

'Only a little.' Karen kept the smile going. 'I suppose it was his looks, his manner, the things he said.'

'What kind of things?'

'You'll find out for yourself one day.'

Regina laughed. 'I look forward to it! I look forward to the baby too,' she added with renewed enthusiasm. 'Shall you choose English names?'

'I doubt if your brother would go along with that.'

It was more than likely true, Karen reflected. She was married to a Brazilian, the child would be a Brazilian. Luiz had already suggested that she apply for citizenship herself, but she had dismissed *that* idea out of hand. The last thing she intended giving up was her nationality.

He'd accepted the refusal with good grace, she had to admit. But then, that was one thing he couldn't lay down the law about.

Reluctant though she'd been to give way to his demand, she'd steered clear of any further one-to-one encounters with Jorge Arroyo, though it proved impossible to avoid him altogether.

'I believed you had more spirit,' he said sadly when they came face to face in La Santa one morning.

'It's called diplomacy,' she defended, seeing no

point in pretending not to know what he was talking about.

'It's called submission,' he countered. 'If you have any independence left at all, you will take coffee with me.'

About to refuse, Karen knew a sudden insurgence. He was right: it was time she showed Luiz she had a mind of her own still.

'All right,' she said.

Jorge gave an approving smile. 'That's better.'

The café he took her to was already well-populated. Karen recognised one or two familiar faces, and knew word would get back to Luiz, but she refused to let it concern her.

'What is it that Luiz has against you, anyway?' she asked when they were seated.

Jorge gave a rueful shrug. 'Regina became attracted to me last year. He believes I encouraged her.'

'And did you?'

He put on a hurt expression. 'I wanted only to paint her. The rest was in her mind only.'

'Tell me about it,' Karen invited.

'There is little to tell,' he said. 'She came to my studio just the three times. I had no notion of her feelings for me until she declared herself. It was difficult to know what to do. I'm not accustomed to dealing with the emotions of teenage girls. Luiz made her tell him what was making her so unhappy. He threatened to kill me.'

'People say all sorts of things under pressure,' Karen responded, trying to view the situation impartially. 'I gather he didn't know about the painting?'

'I hadn't realised that Regina had kept it a secret,' Jorge defended.

Karen studied him for a lengthy moment, uncertain whether to believe him or not. Sixteen was an impressionable age, she had to admit: she'd developed a crush on one of her teachers herself back then.

'I suppose all's well that ends well,' she said at last. 'Regina obviously recovered, and you're still here to tell the tale.'

'It's no tale,' he insisted. 'She held no appeal for me other than as a subject. Perhaps I should have sought Luiz's approval before asking her to sit for me, but I gave it no thought.'

'Whether or not, I think there's enough bad blood between you and Luiz without adding to it,' she said. 'I shouldn't have agreed to this.'

Jorge looked at her scornfully. 'I have no fear of him, but you must do as you see fit, of course.'

It wasn't fear that prompted her, Karen could have told him. She'd accepted the challenge in a belated gesture of defiance against Luiz's dictate, but if he believed Regina had been encouraged by the man, she could understand the objection. If he'd told her why at the time, she would have accepted it.

Only that wasn't Luiz's way, was it? Why should he bother explaining anything?

She could feel eyes following her as she left the café. People who knew both Luiz and Jorge would be aware of the rift between them, even if they didn't know the reason for it. Her being here with the latter had to give rise to speculation.

Regina greeted her reproachfully when she got back to the house.

'I would have come to town with you if I'd known you planned a trip,' she said.

'If you'd been here when I decided, I'd have asked you,' Karen returned mildly. 'Where did you get to?'

'I was helping Carlos change a wheel on the Mercedes,' she said. 'I may have need of such knowledge when I have my own licence next year.'

'Nothing to do with Carlos being such a hunk, of course,' Karen teased.

About to launch an indignant denial, Regina caught her eye and settled for a grin instead.

'He is, isn't he? You won't tell Luiz? He'd get rid of him if he thought I was becoming enamoured.' She sounded suddenly wry. 'I did something very stupid last year, and allowed myself to be dazzled by a man many years older than me. It was fortunate that Luiz found out and put a stop to it, before it became any more than an infatuation on my part.'

It was so strange, Karen thought, that Regina should choose to tell her all this on the same day she'd heard it from Jorge. From the way she *had* told it, it seemed he'd probably been lying through his teeth.

The only way to be sure was to question her further, and the other looked as if she might already be regretting the confidence.

'We've all of us done stupid things at times,' she said comfortingly. 'The best thing is to put it out of mind.'

'It would be easier to do that if I no longer saw him at all.' Regina made an effort to lift her spirits again. 'Have you felt the baby kick yet?'

Karen had to laugh. 'It's far too early for that.'

'But you will let me know the instant it happens?'

'Providing it's not in the middle of the night.' She waited until she was safely in the bedroom before giving way to the impulse that had almost overtaken her downstairs, splaying her fingers across an abdomen still flat and taut. She would be twelve weeks gone or more before there were any really noticeable signs, the gynaecologist had told her. It was barely seven weeks yet, so the stirring she felt had to be in her imagination.

Luiz was turned on by the way she looked now: body slender and supple, breasts high and firm. Would he feel the same way when all that changed?

She whipped her hands away as the door opened. Luiz gazed across at her with quizzically lifted brows.

'You look startled,' he said.

'I was miles away,' she prevaricated. 'I didn't realise you were home.'

'I've been at work in the office for the past two hours. Regina said you'd returned.' He paused, in obvious expectation of some response, gaze sharpening when she failed to make it. 'Is something wrong?'

'You'd better hear it from me before you hear it from someone else,' she said. 'I had coffee with Jorge Arroyo this morning.'

The muscles about the strong mouth tautened ominously. 'I told you—'

'I know what you told me.' Karen kept her tone even. 'I also know *why* you don't want me associating with him. If you'd told me about Regina to start with, I'd have understood.'

Luiz closed the door, face expressionless now. 'I saw no reason to explain my motives.'

'In other words, it should have been enough just to say it.' Karen drew a deep breath, battening down her temper. 'Well, it wasn't.'

'Apparently.' He was angry, but in control of it, the only indication in the slight pinching of his nostrils.

'As I'd doubt that Jorge would have told you about it himself, I gather Regina did.'

'Yes. Although Jorge had already...' Karen broke off, biting her lip.

Luiz gave her a humourless smile. 'Had already claimed to be the innocent victim of a young girl's infatuation, is that what you were about to say?'

'More or less,' she admitted. 'Not that I believed him.'

'That's *something* to be grateful for.'

'There's no need for sarcasm,' she flashed. 'I'm trying to be straight with you. I don't have the slightest interest in Jorge Arroyo!'

'You had coffee with him simply to prove a point?'

'Yes.' She lifted her chin. 'Stupid, I know.'

He surveyed her, lean features relaxing. 'Misguided, perhaps.'

Karen made no move as he came over to her. He took her face between his hands, the way he so often did, tracing the curve of her lips with the ball of his thumb, eyes searching hers. 'No regrets?'

'No regrets,' she echoed.

It was far from the truth. She regretted so many things: winning the money that had brought her here to Brazil in the first place; allowing herself to be overcome by lust; marrying a man she'd known just a few days on the strength of that lust. Because that was all it had ever really been for her, when it came right down to it. She'd been caught up in a fantasy of her own making.

'What is it?' There was a line drawn between the dark brows.

Karen shook herself. Regretted or not, the marriage was a fact. Even if Luiz had been willing to have it dissolved before, he certainly wasn't going to do it now, with the baby on the way.

'I'm feeling a bit homesick, that's all,' she said.

'*This* is your home!' he declared. 'If you return to England at all, it will only be to visit.'

And not for a long time, she thought, reading between the lines.

His kiss drew its usual response from her. That at least hadn't altered. Hopefully it never would.

Luiz's announcement the week before Christmas that they were to visit his mother in Brasilia came as something of a surprise.

'I rather gathered the impression that you were estranged,' Karen said.

'We were for a time,' he admitted. 'She remarried too soon after my father's death for propriety.'

'But you've forgiven her?'

The shrug was brief. 'She's my mother. What else could I do?'

'What about her husband?' Karen asked.

'He's a good enough man. He travels extensively on business, so we may not see him.'

'Your mother does know about me though? I mean, that I'm not Brazilian?'

'She knows.'

They left for Brasilia the following day. It was the first time in several weeks that Karen had been further than a few miles from the ranch.

Driving to the airport, she thought about the journey out when she was still on cloud nine, convinced that she'd found the love of her life. In the physical sense, she probably had, but no matter how fantastic, sex wasn't the be all and end all of a relationship. If she'd never met Luiz she would be waking up in the London flat right about now, with Julie just the other side of the wall and a familiar routine ahead.

'You're very quiet,' Luiz commented, slanting a glance. 'Are you feeling ill?'

Karen seized on the excuse. 'Just a little.'

'Do you wish me to stop the car?'

She shook her head. 'It will pass.'

'Perhaps I should have waited a little longer before making this arrangement,' he said after a moment. 'We can turn back now, if you wish.'

Not looking forward to the coming meeting, she was tempted, but it was best to get it over and done with, she supposed.

'We can't mess your mother around at the last minute,' she said. 'Anyway, it's going off already.'

Luiz winged a smile. 'Women are very resilient.'

Karen suffered a guilty pang. So far she had yet to undergo morning, or any other time of day, sickness. 'We have to be to put up with you men,' she returned, adopting a flippant note.

He laughed. 'Such martyrdom!'

She studied him from the corner of her eye, stirred as always by the sheer masculine impact. She knew his body the way he knew hers, but that was all she really knew of him. It was probably all she would ever really know of him.

'Isn't it though?' she said.

His glance was sharper this time, though he made no comment. Karen could almost hear him putting the brittleness he'd obviously caught in her voice down to her condition. Some of it perhaps was. She felt trapped.

Spread over several square miles, Brasilia was almost surrounded by a vast artificial lake. Luiz's mother lived in a sector of residential dwellings built along the southern end of the lake. The house was set within spacious, landscaped grounds. Long and low, it looked far too large for two people.

The gates were electrified. Luiz spoke briefly into a box set in the side wall, driving through as they opened to bring the hired car to a stop on the wide, stone-laid circle fronting the house.

'What did you say your stepfather does for a living?' Karen asked.

'I didn't say,' Luiz answered. 'He's a cabinet minister, dealing with foreign affairs. Mother met him when she came to Brasilia to visit with friends some weeks after my father's death. They were married within the month.'

'Like mother, like son,' Karen thought, only realising she had actually murmured the words out loud when Luiz stopped in the act of getting from the car to give her a suddenly hardened look.

'There's no comparison!'

'I know.' She made a contrite gesture. 'Our circumstances were completely different.'

The dark eyes failed to soften. 'I'm glad you realise it.'

A man dressed in the dark trousers and white shirt that signified serving staff came from the house. Luiz slid from his seat to answer the respectful greeting, coming round to assist Karen from her place as the man opened the boot to extract their bags.

Karen restrained the urge to say she wasn't yet far enough along to need assistance. Her emotions regarding the baby were still in a state of flux, one minute anticipatory, the next downbeat. Hormones, she supposed.

The house inside was built to the American open plan, with coolly tiled floors winging away in all directions. The furnishings were a little over-elaborate for Karen's tastes, but obviously no expense had been spared. Beyond the sliding glass doors fronting the vast living area could be seen a broad covered lanai, and beyond that a free-form swimming pool complete with waterfall.

Cristina Belsamo rose from a brocade chair. Considering Luiz's age, she had to be in her fifties, yet she looked no more than the mid-forties. She was both beautiful and elegant in her designer dress of cream silk, her luxuriant dark hair piled high, but the smile on her lips was not reflected in her eyes.

She greeted her son in Portuguese, switching to a somewhat formalised English to address Karen herself.

'You are very lovely, but I would have expected no less. You must be weary from the journey. You would no doubt like to rest before dinner.'

It was more of a command than a suggestion, Karen thought. Not much of a welcome anyway. It was on the tip of her tongue to say she'd much prefer to take a swim, but she bit it back. She hadn't a suit with her, in any case, and this was no place to go skinny-dipping.

'That's very considerate of you,' she said instead.

'You have the blue suite,' Cristina told Luiz, adding something in Portuguese too fast for Karen to even take a guess at translation.

He made no answer in either language, simply indicating that Karen should accompany him. His expression was unrevealing, though she sensed something simmering beneath the surface.

The guest suites lay down a side corridor. Three of them, counting the doors beyond the one Luiz opened. Blue was certainly the colour: carpet, drapes, bedspreads, all toning shades against off-white walls. Twin beds, Karen noted: Cristina's way of expressing her feelings about the marriage, perhaps. She at least had married another Brazilian, not a foreigner.

Their bags had already been deposited on stands at the foot of each bed. Had they not been locked, Karen suspected they would have been unpacked too by now.

'Leave that,' Luiz said as she made a move towards her own bag. 'You need to rest.'

'I'm not in the least tired,' she retorted. 'Will you please stop treating me like an invalid?'

'I have no intention of treating you like an invalid,' he denied levelly. 'Now, or at any other time. You must naturally do as you feel able.'

Karen caught herself up, already regretting the tartness. 'Sorry,' she said. 'That was uncalled for. I just…' She broke off, spreading her hands in a helpless gesture. 'Maybe I am tired.'

His expression relaxed a little. Coming forward, he tilted her chin with a finger to receive his kiss.

'I'll be with you shortly,' he said. 'My mother wishes to speak with me.'

To express her disapproval face to face, no doubt, Karen reflected. Not that there was anything the woman could do about it.

She unpacked both bags while Luiz was gone. With no clear idea of how long they would be staying, or what they might be doing, she had allowed for all eventualities. If Edigar Balsamo was away, it was unlikely that Cristina would be entertaining friends. That would be a relief in itself. Dealing with her attitude was going to be bad enough. Facing others of the same viewpoint she could do without.

The sun went down in a blaze of glory, backlighting the clouds spreading out from the horizon. Beyond the pool and outlying grounds lay an uninterrupted view of the lake's southern reaches. Cabinet Ministers must be pretty well-paid to afford a place like this, Karen reflected. Of the two, she much preferred Guavada.

Luiz looked distinctly rattled when he eventually returned. Karen forbore from asking the obvious question. Assuming that dinner would be at the same time as Guavada, there were still a couple of hours to go. She knew one sure way of passing the time pleasurably for them both.

A smile overcame the tension about the strong mouth as he read the message in her eyes.

'You,' he said, 'are a rare woman!'

'For an Englishwoman, you mean?' she murmured as he drew her to him and heard his low laugh.

'For any nationality!'

The lovemaking was incredible as always. Luiz never rushed things, nor allowed her to do so. As always, when she was in his arms, she wanted to be nowhere else. When she was in his arms, the whole world could go to hell for all she cared. In his arms, she had no inhibitions: teasing him with caresses that drew him to the very brink; offering herself to him with wanton abandonment when he in turn aroused her to fever pitch.

'I heard that pregnancy can turn a woman against sex in the initial stages,' he murmured when they lay entwined after a climax that robbed them of just about every ounce of energy. 'I can only be thankful for my good fortune.'

He lifted his head to look into her eyes, the amber lights deep in the darkness of his drawing her in. 'You fulfil my every desire!'

At this moment perhaps, she thought. 'And you mine,' she murmured back, because it was expected of her. 'You're a lover without equal!'

His smile was brief. 'You have no comparison. Nor will you while I draw breath,' he added on a suddenly fiercer note. 'You're mine, and mine alone!'

Possession, not love, came the fading thought as he claimed her once more.

They were in Brasilia just three days in total. Three days that seemed more like three months. Cristina was courteous, but no more than that. Nor was she likely to soften, Karen judged. In her view, Luiz had betrayed his race by marrying out of it.

A handsome man in his early sixties, Edigar Belsamo put in a brief appearance that first evening. Although he made an effort to extend a welcome, he obviously found the situation difficult. Karen was unsurprised when he announced that he had to leave again the following morning. She only wished she could do the same.

Luiz spent the whole of the next day showing her round the capital with its ultra modern plazas and buildings. Karen would have preferred to explore on foot, but with temperatures in the lower eighties and little shade, few people walked anywhere.

'I'd hate to live here,' she said over lunch at one of the city's top hotels. 'It's so huge!'

'So is London,' Luiz returned, 'but you lived there.'

Nostalgia swamped her for a moment, totally disregarding the times she'd wished she could swap city living for somewhere in the countryside. 'It's not the same,' she said.

He regarded her quizzically. 'Apart from the architecture, in what way is it different from any other city?'

'It has soul. A history that goes back hundreds of years, not just a few decades! If you'd ever visited it, you'd know what I'm talking about.'

'You must give me the guided tour.'

Karen gazed at him in silence for a moment, unable to decide whether he meant what he seemed to be implying, or was just making noises.

'When?' she asked, opting for the former.

His shrug was easy. 'Perhaps in a year or so when the child is old enough to be left.'

If he had his way, she would probably be pregnant again by then, she reflected, recalling what he'd said about this not being their only child. Not that she had any quarrel with that. She'd have loved siblings of her own.

The best thing might be not to go back at all. What was the point? Her life was here now. Perhaps not quite as perfect as she had first envisioned, but hardly a bad one.

'What are your thoughts?' Luiz asked curiously, watching the play of expressions across her face.

'I was wishing we were home,' she said impulsively, surprising herself because it was the first time she had thought of Guavada in that light. 'I'm sure your mother would have no objection if we leave tomorrow.'

Something flickered deep down in the dark eyes. 'I have matters I must attend to tomorrow.'

He made no attempt to enlarge on that statement. Business matters, Karen supposed. The thought of spending the day alone with her mother-in-law was far from appealing.

Cristina had an engagement herself in the morning. Karen spent it out on the lanai with a book. Luiz hadn't said how long his affairs might take. She hoped he'd be back before his mother returned.

He wasn't. Cristina came in around one-thirty, and the two them ate lunch together. Conversation was minimal, the atmosphere frigid. Karen could finally stand it no longer.

'I realise you totally disapprove of me as a suitable wife for your son,' she said, 'but I'm *his* choice. Can't you accept that?'

There was no softening of expression in the older woman's eyes. 'I will never accept it!' she stated. 'He did this to punish me!'

Karen looked at her in some bewilderment. 'Punish you?'

'For the insult I gave to his father's memory.'

'Oh, come on!' Karen could scarcely believe she was serious. 'He'd hardly go that far!'

'You think you know my son better than I do myself?' Cristina gave a short, humourless laugh. 'You have a lot to learn about him. He could have had his choice of bride from among those fit to bear the name. Why else, if it were not to hurt me, would he choose one he knew I could never approve?'

'He told me his father died some years ago,' Karen returned. 'Why would he wait this long to get back at you?'

The laugh came again. 'He had first to find someone who fulfilled his physical needs too.'

It could quite possibly be true, Karen thought, feeling a dull ache in the pit of her stomach. She already knew that Luiz didn't love her—at least, not what she called love. But then, she didn't love him either.

Yes, you do, whispered the small voice at the back of her mind. Stop hiding from it!

She swallowed thickly, searching for something—*anything*—to say to the woman.

'You're entitled to believe whatever you want to believe,' she got out. 'The fact remains, I'm Luiz's wife and I'm carrying his child. Your first grandchild.'

'You think so?' Cristina's expression registered derision. 'As I said, you have a lot to learn.'

Karen studied her uncertainly, grappling with the implications. 'What are you trying to tell me?'

For a moment the older woman seemed to hesitate, then she lifted her shoulders. 'You believe Luiz is conducting some business affairs today, but you are wrong. He is visiting his son.'

How long Karen just sat there she couldn't have said. Her mind was in turmoil. 'You're lying,' she whispered at length.

'Why would I lie about such a thing?' the other woman demanded. 'Do you think I am any more proud to have a bastard grandchild than I shall be to have one of mixed blood?'

'Why…' Karen cleared her throat and tried again. 'Why didn't he marry the mother?'

A shutter came down suddenly in her mother-in-law's eyes. 'She is not of our class. I refuse to discuss the matter further,' she added flatly. 'He does duty by the child, that is all you need to know.'

And what did he do for the mother? Karen wondered. She hurt as though she'd been kicked. She got to her feet, unsurprised by the shakiness in her limbs. 'I'm going to take a siesta.'

The expression that flitted across Cristina's face could have been shame, though Karen doubted it.

'If you are wise, you will say nothing to Luiz of this,' the woman said.

If she were wise, she wouldn't be in this position to start with, Karen could have answered. She didn't because the words would have stuck in her throat.

The bedroom was cool and dim, the window blinds slanted against the sun's rays. She lay down on her bed fully clothed, gazing blindly at the shadowed ceiling.

Her hand moved of its own accord to caress her abdomen. Not Luiz's first child after all: that honour belonged to a boy born the wrong side of the blanket through no fault of his own. Under English law, he would have the same claim as any legitimate issue, but this wasn't England.

Not of our class, Cristina had said of the mother. Marriageable she may not be in Luiz's eyes too, but she would certainly be good-looking. There was every chance that the two of them were in bed together right now.

The pain went deep. What she was going to do she couldn't begin to think—didn't want to think. It was all too much to cope with.

Emotionally drained, she finally fell asleep, waking with a jerk when Luiz came into the room.

'Are you feeling unwell?' he asked concernedly.

Karen made a valiant effort to pull herself together as memory came flooding in. 'Just tired,' she said. 'What time is it?'

'Ten minutes past five,' he answered, glancing at his watch. 'I'm sorry to have been away so long.'

The time to fling accusations was now, but the words wouldn't come. 'Busy day?' she said instead.

'Very,' he agreed. 'I've told my mother we'll be leaving in the morning.'

'Good.' She faked a yawn, unable to stand much more for the moment. 'Do you mind if I go back to sleep for a while?'

He came over to the bed, dropping to sit on the mattress edge to bend and put his lips to her temple. 'You look pale,' he observed. 'Are you sure there's nothing wrong?'

Another opportunity, but she couldn't bring herself to take it. She steeled herself when he ran the back of his fingers gently down her cheek. Even knowing what she knew made little difference to her responses. She wanted him the way she had always wanted him. No doubt he had the same effect on his mistress.

'I told you, I'm just tired,' she said, trying to keep a level tone.

He considered her for a moment, obviously not wholly deceived, then he patted her cheek again and got to his feet. 'Have all the rest you need, of course. I'll take a change of clothing to another room so that I don't disturb you.'

She watched through slitted lids as he gathered what he needed, letting out a pent-up breath on a long-drawn sigh when he went from the room. She should have faced him with what she had learned, she knew. She hadn't because deep down she didn't want to hear him admit it, didn't want to see the guilt in his eyes.

He would have counted on his mother keeping her own council, considering her feelings towards his illegitimate son. Cristina was unlikely to confess her betrayal, so why rock the boat? For the sake of the child growing inside her, if nothing else, she had to put the whole affair aside.

CHAPTER NINE

THE journey back to Guavada was passed for the most part in silence. His conversational overtures unproductive, Luiz ran out of patience in the end.

'Do you find pregnancy such a toil that even words are too much of a burden?' he asked in the car. 'I accept—as I accepted last night—that there will be times now when you feel too physically tired for lovemaking, but you can surely summon the strength to talk!

'I didn't think what you were saying just now called for any in-depth response,' Karen retorted, drawing a narrowed glance.

'I doubt if you were even listening to what I was saying just now. You've been in a strange mood all day, in fact.'

'I'm a woman,' she returned, trying to make light of it. 'We're a moody species. You men just have to learn to live with it, I'm afraid.'

'Not this man,' came the less than humorous reply. 'If you have some grievance I prefer to hear it.'

The accusation trembled once more on her lips, but was held back by a stronger instinct. 'What grievance could I possibly have?' she said instead. 'You give me everything a woman could want.' She forced herself to reach out a hand to touch his thigh, to put a smile on her lips. 'Sorry for being such a grump.'

The answering smile was somewhat restrained. 'You're forgiven. Just don't let it happen too often.'

Karen kept a tight rein on the tart retort. If she let fly now it would all come out, and what good would it do in the end? She could demand that he give up all physical contact with the other woman and her child, but it was unlikely that he'd agree never to see his son again.

While it pained her to know that the baby she carried wasn't his first-born, she could somehow stomach that more easily than the probability that he still had a relationship with the other woman. She'd turned from him last night because she couldn't rid herself of the images. Images that still persisted, although what excuse she would use tonight she had no idea.

The sun was already setting when they reached Guavada. Regina greeted them with her customary enthusiasm. She'd so missed her companionship, she told Karen.

'How did you find my mother?' she asked when the two of them were alone for a few minutes.

Karen kept her tone as easy as she could. 'I doubt if we'll ever be great friends.'

'I was afraid of that.' Regina sounded rueful. 'She had what she believed would be the ideal wife for Luiz already chosen years ago. There have been others too, but Luiz favoured none of them. You must not allow her rejection to hurt you. She would have been the same over anyone he'd chosen for himself.'

Perhaps not so much if he'd chosen one of his own countrywomen, Karen reflected. Right now, her mother-in-law's feelings weren't of importance to her. She had far more pressing matters on her mind.

Unable to cast those matters aside, she slipped out on to the veranda after dinner for a breath of fresh air. The night air was deliciously cool on her skin. Seated on the swing couch, she contemplated the moonlit landscape. Guavada had grown on her, she had to admit that now. If it weren't for what she knew, she could even consider it home. If she truly didn't love Luiz, none of what she'd learned would hurt as much, she was sure. The question was, how did she cope with that hurt?

'I was speaking with Cristina earlier,' said Beatriz from the doorway. There was an odd note in her voice. 'She tells me you know about the boy.'

Karen didn't turn her head. 'So I know about the boy.'

The pause was lengthy, the atmosphere charged. 'Are you going to tell Luiz that you know?' Beatriz finally asked on the same odd note.

'I see no reason to.' Karen kept her tone level with an effort. 'It happened before we met.'

'You are very tolerant. More than I would be myself in such circumstances.' The other woman sounded almost sympathetic.

'We're very different people,' Karen returned, not trusting the sympathy for a moment. 'Concentrate on your own marriage, and leave me to deal with mine.'

'*My* marriage is secure in every way,' retorted her sister-in-law, dropping back into character. 'Yours is dependent on the way you look. Luiz is a man to whom a woman's looks are all important. Should she lose them, he would have little interest left.'

She was telling her nothing she didn't already suspect, Karen acknowledged. If she didn't look the way she did, Luiz would never have even noticed her that day in Rio. It boded ill for the future.

Beatriz disappeared back indoors, leaving her to contemplate that future with growing despondency. It took the gathering ache in her lower back to bring her back to the present. She eased her position, but the ache remained, spreading now to her abdomen and increasing in intensity to a gripping pain.

The realisation of what was happening struck her with mind-numbing force. She clutched herself, as if it might be stopped by application of pressure, knowing it was a useless gesture. Nature held the upper hand.

'So here you are!' Luiz exclaimed, appearing round the corner of the veranda. 'I was beginning to—'

He broke off abruptly as he took in her position and drawn expression. 'What is it?'

'The baby,' she got out through clenched teeth. 'I'm losing the baby!'

Things happened in a blur from there. Luiz carried her into the house, an ambulance was called, and she was transported to the nearby clinic, where vain attempts were made to stay the process. Karen suffered through it all in silence, the sense of loss too deep for words. She knew Luiz was there with her, but there was no comfort to be found.

He was at the bedside when she awoke from a sedated sleep, strain etched deep on the olive features.

'I'm sorry,' she said tonelessly.

He took her hand, raising it to his lips. There were no amber lights in the dark eyes. 'If the fault lies with anyone at all, it must be mine for taking you on an unnecessary journey.'

'Do the doctors say that?' she asked.

'No,' he admitted. 'They tell me it just happens this way sometimes for no apparent reason.'

But not to his mistress, she thought. He should have married her, if only for his son's sake. The boy had more right to the Andrade name than any child she might have had.

'They also tell me,' he went on, 'that there's no reason why you shouldn't carry a child to full-term in the future.'

'Nothing to stop us trying again then.'

'But not immediately.' His tone was steady. 'You need time to recover.'

'Whatever you think,' she said. She took her hand from him to push back the sheet and press herself upright. 'I just want to get out of here.'

Christmas came and went quietly. With the miscarriage almost two weeks behind her, Karen insisted that celebrations for the New Year were not curtailed.

Open to all and sundry, the Guavada barbecue was renowned. It began at midday, to finish when the last reveller departed. Not even the hour-long summer rainstorm could dampen the party spirit. People either took shelter until it passed over, or simply stood around in it, depending on age. With the temperature hovering in the mid-eighties, there was little danger of catching a chill.

Luiz took over one of the grills himself after the rain stopped. Karen watched him as he doled out sizzling steaks to the seemingly never-ending line, exchanging repartee. Devastated though he'd been by the miscarriage, he'd proved a tower of strength the past two weeks. It was difficult to equate the man he appeared to be with the man she now knew him to be.

'The master cooks well for us,' said a voice she didn't recognise.

She turned to view the man who had spoken, the smile ready on her lips fading a little as she met bold dark eyes. One of the ranch hands, judging from his clothing, she guessed. Young and good-looking, he appraised her in turn, his expression only too easily read.

'Yes, he does,' she replied in the same language. 'You work for him?'

He inclined his head, his gaze discomfiting. 'I am Lucio Fernandas. You are even more beautiful than it is said. Luiz is a lucky man!'

With her command of the language still in its infancy, and his speech fast, Karen had a struggle to translate but she got the gist. The words themselves were innocuous enough, the look accompanying them far from it.

Dona Ferrez came to her rescue, drawing her away before she could summon any kind of reply.

'What was he saying to you?' asked the older woman.

'Nothing much,' Karen answered, reluctant to make any fuss over what amounted to no more than a leer. She'd been treated to worse than that back home in England.

'Luiz would not like it that he speak with you,' Dona declared.

'Then we won't tell him,' Karen said lightly. 'Do you think anyone will think it rude of me if I take a bit of a siesta?'

'Of course they will not! You must not tire yourself. I will tell Luiz where you are.'

Karen turned for the house as Dona headed for the grills, almost running into Beatriz. The other made no attempt to speak, her regard narrowed as if in contemplation. Whatever was brewing in the woman's head, Karen was past caring. All she wanted at present was to lay her head on a soft pillow and sleep.

She awoke to the feather-light touch of lips on hers. Luiz smiled at her bemused expression.

'I thought it time to come and check on you,' he said.

'How long have I been asleep?' she asked.

'More than two hours. Some of our guests have already left, but the rest seem prepared to stay out the rest of the day. Do you feel strong enough to rejoin them, or shall I ask them all to depart?'

'Don't do that.' Karen sat up, swinging her legs to the floor as Luiz rose to his feet. 'Give me fifteen minutes to have a shower and change my clothes, and I'll be down.'

'You're sure you feel up to it?' he insisted.

She felt anything but, only she wasn't about to admit it. 'Quite sure,' she said.

Luiz drew her to her feet and into his arms, holding her close for a moment or two. 'There can be other babies,' he consoled. 'There's no haste. For now, we'll rest content with each other.'

Until he felt moved to visit the woman who *had* provided him with a child, thought Karen hollowly.

The last of the revellers finally weaved their way homewards around ten, by which time even Regina had had enough.

'I would like my birthday celebration at Café Lamas,' she declared, naming the town's top restaurant. 'Eighteen is a very special age.'

'It is indeed,' agreed Luiz. 'I'll make the arrangements.'

'And a car of my own?' she suggested.

He smiled. 'Reaching the age of authority to hold a licence is only a beginning. When you know how to drive a car, I may consider it.'

'You can teach me, the way you taught Karen.'

'When exactly *is* your birthday?' Karen asked, forced to smile herself as she caught Luiz's dry glance.

'The thirteenth of January.' Regina pulled a face. 'Not a nice date on which to be born.'

Hardly an unlucky one for her, considering what she'd been born into, Karen reflected. A life of leisure until she married, and even then it would be to a man rich enough to keep her in the style to which she was accustomed.

Not that she had anything to complain about in that sense herself.

She left Luiz to share a nightcap with his brother. Beatriz followed her from the room.

'I saw you with Lucio Fernandas earlier,' she said. 'As did others. It was fortunate that Luiz did not.'

'Why?' Karen asked. 'Are the ranch hands considered too far down the social scale?'

'For his wife to exchange banter with, yes.'

Karen opened her mouth to deny the allegation, cutting off the words in the certain knowledge that Beatriz would pay little heed. 'Your concern does you credit,' she said instead, and continued on her way.

She was in bed, though far from sleep, when Luiz came up. He had exercised the utmost forbearance since the miscarriage, although it couldn't have been easy, she knew, for a man of his appetites to hold himself in check for so long.

Watching him as he undressed, she wanted him again, desperately enough to override everything else. She reached for him the moment he slid into the bed, bringing him to instant arousal.

Even then, he restrained himself long enough to

take measures against conception. Karen made no protest. The last thing she wanted was another pregnancy.

Listening to his steady breathing later, feeling the muscular strength of his arms about her, she could almost feel sorry for the woman who would only know this on infrequent occasions. Sorry too for the boy who would grow up barely knowing his father at all. She might not have everything she desired herself, but she had so much. Could she begrudge the two of them so little?

The days slid by. Regina's birthday came and went with all the appropriate observance. Karen gave her a course of professional driving lessons to go with the sleek little sports model Luiz came up with despite all he'd said.

Life went along much the same as it had before the trip to Brasilia. A good life in most respects. Without Beatriz around, it might have been possible to come to terms with the situation, but the woman lost no opportunity to taunt her with the knowledge they shared whenever they were alone together.

Had she no pride, that she'd stay with a man who led a double life? she would jeer. Did she really believe he had any real depth of feeling for her?

Karen didn't believe it, but it still hurt to hear it put into words. Perhaps Beatriz was right, she told herself. She should have more pride. She still had enough left from the lottery win to pay her passage back to England. All it took was the will.

If she hadn't been so emotionally off-balance she would have seen what a crazy idea it was—that the only realistic course was to bring the whole affair out into the open—but it continued to fester at the back of her mind.

It took the photograph Beatriz showed her of mother and son to precipitate matters. Karen had known the woman would be beautiful, but she had expected a woman, not a teenage girl who could surely have been no more than sixteen when she had become pregnant.

How could Luiz live with himself? she thought numbly. How could *she* continue to live with him after this?

He'd left early without waking her that morning. Mind blanked of everything but the urge to get away, she left Beatriz and went upstairs to throw a few things haphazardly into a suitcase. Her passport was to hand. She stuffed that into a bag, along with what ready cash she could find. It wouldn't be enough to get her where she was going, and she'd never bothered with a cheque book, so she'd just have to use the credit card Luiz had provided her with to purchase a ticket home. What she would do when she got there, she didn't even think about.

Beatriz had disappeared. Regina had gone to visit a friend, and Raymundo was out somewhere too. Even the staff seemed to have vanished. She took the car she'd first learned to drive in, keeping her gaze fixed straight ahead as she headed out past the house that had been her home for the past months. That part of her life was finished with.

The drive to São Paulo was the longest she had undertaken on her own. The realisation, on reaching the Congonhas airport at last, that it only handled domestic flights, was dismaying. It meant retrieving the car from the car park where she'd left it, and driving many further kilometres to the international airport on the other side of the city.

She could take a bus to Guarulhas, a helpful counter

clerk advised her. He even offered to check if there were any London flights scheduled, although he didn't hold out much hope of securing a seat at such short notice.

He was right about that. All London flights were booked solid for the next three weeks. There was one seat going spare on a flight from Rio at seven, he said, consulting the computer readout once more. He could get her on the three-thirty shuttle, which should give her plenty of time to cross to Rio's international airport.

Still in the grip of the same compulsion, Karen was ready to do whatever it took. She paid for both flights with the platinum card. An expensive detour, but Luiz could afford it.

It was a lengthy wait for the shuttle. The plane was full, the noise from a crowd of excited schoolchildren overpowering. Karen closed her eyes as they lifted off, only now beginning to come to her senses a little. Luiz wasn't going to just let her go like this. She was his wife, his property. Wherever she went, he'd find her, there was little doubt of that.

Well, let him! she thought resolutely. Once out of the country, she'd be safe from any attempt to force her back. If he wouldn't divorce her, she'd divorce him, however long it took.

The man occupying the seat at her side said something unintelligible and got to his feet, allowing someone else to slide into the seat. Some kind of mix up, she supposed.

'Fortune smiles on me!' declared the newcomer.

Karen opened her eyes to view the man in startled recognition, unable to believe that Lucio Fernandas was on the plane too.

'What are you doing here?' she asked blankly.

He flashed his teeth in a grin. 'Like you, I go to Rio. I have money. Much money! I can give you a good time.'

'Not in a thousand years!' she said in English.

If he didn't understand the words, he understood the meaning. The smile disappeared. Karen had no idea what his response was, although it certainly wasn't polite. She was thankful when he returned the seat to its original occupier.

She turned her attention to the window in order to avoid the man's obvious curiosity. The coincidence apart, there was something very odd about Fernandas being on the plane at all. She had no idea what the Guavada hands earned, but would have doubted it was enough to allow vacations in one of the most expensive cities in the world.

It was none of her business, anyway, she concluded. She had more important things on her mind.

Up to now she hadn't given a thought to what she was going to do on landing in London. Finding somewhere to stay would be a first priority. If Luiz cancelled the credit card—which was a possibility she hadn't taken into account—she'd be in real trouble. She could hardly turn up at Julie's door like some waif and stray.

It would be far more sensible to turn back and sort the whole thing out at source, she acknowledged, but common sense had played no part from the beginning of her whole relationship with Luiz. For better or for worse, she'd made her choice.

She took care on landing to steer well clear of any further encounter with Lucio Fernandas. Buses ran to the international airport but she'd be best taking a taxi, the counter clerk had told her. With two and a half hours still to go before the London flight, she should be fine, providing she could get transportation fairly quickly.

There were people milling around outside the concourse. Confused, Karen hesitated on the edge of the busy service road. That must be the taxi rank across there, she thought, catching a flash of yellow through the press. If she stepped lively…

CHAPTER TEN

KAREN caught sight of her watch as she slid the photograph back into the drawer where she had found it. She felt quite numb at present.

The money Lucio Fernandas had boasted of could only have come from Beatriz: she must have sent the man off post-haste to back up the story she had given Luiz. It suggested pre-planning: counting on the effect the photograph would have on a mind already primed. Considering the circumstances, she couldn't possibly have known about the Rio flight—that must have been his own idea—but it had certainly lent credence to the story.

Luiz was probably with his mistress right now. At this hour, his son would be in bed, leaving the two of them to catch up on the long weeks since their last meeting. It was back to square one, facing the problem her mind had solved once by returning her to a time before the lottery win that had begun it all. As that was unlikely to happen again, she had to deal with it this time. How, she couldn't even begin to think.

There was no sign of Beatriz when she emerged from the office. Not that she'd expected her to be hanging around. In no frame of mind to face anyone, she headed for the privacy of the bedroom.

It took sight of the bed she'd shared with Luiz these past weeks to unlock her emotions. When she thought of the way she'd gone to him that night—begged him to make love to her—she almost retched. To be disillusioned once was bad enough, but to go through it twice!

She was sitting by the window, still fully dressed, when Regina came up to find out what had happened to her.

'Are you feeling ill?' she asked anxiously.

'Just a bit off-colour, that's all,' Karen assured her.

'Do you think you might be pregnant again?' her sister-in-law ventured.

'No!' she snapped, immediately regretting it as she saw the expression on the younger girl's face. 'I doubt it,' she amended on a milder note. 'Sorry for being such a bear. I've got a really bad headache. Would you mind fetching me a couple of painkillers?'

Regina made for the bathroom with a readiness that made Karen ashamed, returning with the pills and a glass of water. 'If there is anything else I can do for you, you know you have only to ask,' she said.

'I know.' Karen forced a smile. 'Thanks.'

The headache was real enough, though she doubted if the aspirin would have any effect. Alone again, she tried to come to some kind of decision about where she went from here, but she was too weary in spirit. Luiz had said he'd be gone two or three days, so there was no immediate pressure.

She spent a restless night, getting up heavy-eyed and depressed. With no appetite, she went down to breakfast only to set Regina's mind at rest.

The others were already at the table. Beatriz looked unusually subdued. Probably realising the danger she'd placed herself in by allowing her animus to overcome her last night, Karen reflected. Luiz would be merciless when he knew she'd lied about Lucio Fernandas.

If he believed it, that was. She had no actual proof that Beatriz had plotted the whole thing.

'You're evil, do you know that?' she accused the other woman when she got her alone. 'Stupid too. If you'd left things the way they were, I might never have known what you were capable of!'

'A mistake, I admit,' Beatriz returned without remorse. 'Although regaining your memory really changes very little when I come to consider. The fact that Lucio was on the same plane is still enough to condemn you.'

'Not if I can prove that you paid him to follow me,' Karen flashed back, bringing a sneer to her sister-in-law's lips.

'And how would you do that?'

'Luiz has someone out searching for him. He'll get to the truth!'

That gave Beatriz pause for a moment, but only for a moment. 'First he has to find him,' she said. 'What should concern you more is the secret he's kept from you all these months. How does it feel to know that he's with Margarita and Maurice this moment?'

It felt, Karen thought, like a sword through her chest!

'I'll deal with that in my own time and my own way,' she said. 'I'll leave *him* to deal with you.'

Beatriz eyed her with a certain calculation. 'Will telling Luiz you recovered your memory really gain you anything?'

Nothing at all, she was bound to admit. It would still be her word against Beatriz's with respect to Lucio Fernandas, with the fact that they'd both been on the Rio flight, coincidence though it must have been, weighing against her. And she would still have to face his duplicity.

'Why not just leave things the way they are?' Beatriz pursued, sensing her hesitation. 'Do you think Luiz will cast Margarita and her son aside for you? *You* have his name. That is what matters.'

'To you, maybe,' Karen returned.

'To any woman.' Beatriz paused. 'We might even become friends ourselves in time. Think on it.'

She moved away before Karen could reply. Not that she was in any doubt about her answer. She'd as soon put her trust in a rattlesnake!

The day dragged on interminably. Regina was like a cat on hot bricks waiting for Miran to call. She grew ever more despondent as the hours passed. With a good idea of what was coming, Karen had little desire to keep the appointment she'd made with the man herself.

She told no one she was going out after lunch. Miran was waiting at the corner of the central square in La Santa. He got into the car quickly, enabling her to drive on almost without stopping.

'It's good of you to come,' he declared. 'I'm concerned that Regina may have taken my attentions to mean more than I intended them to mean.'

'What makes you think that?' Karen asked cautiously.

'The things she said at luncheon yesterday. She spoke of you and Luiz, and the way the two of you knew immediately that you wished to spend the rest of your lives together. She said that Luiz could have no complaint that we felt the same way about each other.' He spread his hands. 'I gave her no cause to believe such a thing!'

'You paid her a lot of attention the other night,' Karen responded, shelving her own problems for the present in sympathy with her sister-in-law's coming disillusionment.

'No more than I would pay any beautiful girl!' he protested. 'It was never my intention to suggest anything more than admiration for that beauty. You think she may have spoken with Luiz already?' he added anxiously.

Karen gave him a disgusted glance, aware now of the main concern.

'Luiz is in Brasilia,' she said. 'He knows nothing of this.' She paused, marshalling her reserves. 'I think you should be more careful of what you say and how you say it in future. I also think you should have had the decency to make your feelings clear when you met yesterday, instead of allowing Regina to go on imagining you shared her emotions.'

The handsome features took on a piqued expression. 'You would have had me embarrass her that way?'

'You could have found some way of letting her down gently if you'd really tried, instead of relying on someone else to put her straight. That's what you are relying on, isn't it?'

'It's best that she hear it from someone close to her who can offer comfort,' he agreed shamelessly.

Karen curled a scornful lip. 'Best for you, you mean. I think it might be a good idea if you go back to São Paulo today. I'm sure you can find some adequate excuse.'

'Perhaps so,' he said. He studied her for a moment, taking in the pure lines of her face, the silken sheen of her hair, his expression altering to one she was only too familiar with. 'You're very beautiful yourself.'

Karen turned a deaf ear. 'I'll take you back to the square.'

She was glad to have shut of him. Regina was going to suffer when he failed to get in touch again, but she'd get over it. The way *she* would have got over Luiz if she'd had the sense to return home all those months ago.

It was almost five o'clock when she got back to the house. Walking into the hall to see Luiz descending the stairs was a shock that left her momentarily lost for words.

'You look as if you'd seen a ghost,' he commented drily.

'I wasn't expecting to see you for another couple of days,' she managed.

'My business was completed in less time than anticipated.' His appraisal too keen for comfort, he added, 'I arrived home over an hour ago. Where have you been?'

'Just driving around,' she said. 'If I'd known, of course—'

'You would have been here to greet me,' he finished for her. The dark brows lifted as she continued to stand there. 'So, do I not get a welcome now?'

She went to him reluctantly, steeling herself for his kiss. Her toned down response drew a speculative look.

'I think there are things we need to discuss,' he said.

'About what?' she asked.

His lips twisted. 'About the fact that I did you an injustice where Miran Villota is concerned. I'd seen you watching him during the evening. When you appeared to defend him later, I believed you were drawn to him.' He held her close again, pressing his lips to her temple. 'I can't bear for you to be drawn to *any* other man!'

But it was all right for him to want another woman, she thought. Even more than one, for all she knew! She should do what she should have done weeks ago, and expose him for the hypocrite he was!

She didn't because she couldn't. Because, in spite of it all, she admitted wryly, he still exercised the same power. Just being here close to him now, she wanted him. When it came to matter over mind, it was just no contest.

'I've no interest in Miran Villota,' she said.

'I know that now. I must learn to curb my possessiveness.' He kissed her again and released her, his smile a caress in itself. 'I have much to make up for.'

He'd expect to do that tonight in bed, of course. That gave her five or six hours to come to some final decision. Either she faced him with the truth, or she did as Beatriz had suggested and settled for what she had.

The evening stretched interminably. Regina was so unusually quiet Luiz was drawn to ask if she was suffering some ailment. He looked unconvinced when she denied it, though he didn't pursue the subject.

A little on edge to begin with, Beatriz relaxed as time went on, contempt in her eyes when she looked Karen's way. She was assuming too much too soon, Karen could have told her; the decision was still to be made.

Regina singled her out at the first opportunity, her lovely young face downcast.

'Miran didn't call,' she said. 'Do you think I should call him?'

Karen hesitated, not at all sure she was capable of

handling other problems in addition to her own right now.

'I think it would be best to wait and see,' she advised at length.

Her sister-in-law's face clouded even further. 'You think I was too hasty, don't you?' she said miserably. 'That I took his interest in me for more than it was?'

It was sometimes necessary to be cruel to be kind, Karen reflected, and took the plunge. 'It's possible, yes. Men like Miran are not the kind to put any trust in.'

'But he was so wonderful to me!' Regina burst out. 'If he felt nothing for me, why did he allow me to believe he did?'

'I'm sure he did feel something for you.'

'But not enough.' Tears were threatening. 'Why did he not stop me from making a fool of myself!'

'Perhaps he just couldn't find it in himself to hurt you,' Karen murmured.

Regina dashed the back of her hand across her eyes. 'The hurt is no less now than it would have been then. I'll never trust any man again!'

'They're not all the same,' Karen comforted, wishing she could be convinced of that herself. 'You've all the time in the world to find the right one.'

She'd thought Luiz engrossed in conversation with his brother. Looking up to find his gaze fixed on the two of them was disconcerting. He would naturally want to know what Regina was upset about, but his sister would be even more mortified than she already was to have him know about it.

Regina compounded speculation by eating little at dinner. She excused herself with a plea of tiredness the moment the meal was finished, and departed for bed. Karen toyed with the idea of following her up to offer more comfort, but decided that she was probably best left alone for now.

She had her own troubles still to deal with anyway. As time crept on, she grew ever more uncertain of which way to go. Her heart almost broke through her ribcage when Luiz suggested it was time they retired for the night.

'Why was Regina weeping?' he asked as they mounted the stairs.

'It's private,' Karen answered. 'Woman to woman.'

Luiz gave her a shrewd glance 'Nothing to do with Miran Villota?'

'I thought *I* was the one supposed to be interested in him?' she responded.

'A mistake for which I already apologised,' he said without inflection. 'I don't need to be reminded of it. I trust the distress has no physical basis?'

Further denials were useless, Karen decided resignedly. 'Of course not,' she said. 'Regina would never allow herself to be taken in that far.'

'It can happen.' They had reached their door. Luiz opened it, ushering her through ahead of him. 'I believed she had learned to be a little more selective.'

He was referring to the affair with Jorge Arroyo, Karen guessed. Something Regina could have told her about since the memory loss, of course, but she refrained from comment.

'You wish to use the bathroom first?' he asked, already unbuttoning his shirt.

She seized on the chance to extend the decision time, knowing she was only putting off the inevitable.

She always took a shower before going to bed. Tonight, there was no stimulation to be found.

Her mind was going round in circles. She couldn't ask Luiz to give up his son, but she could demand that he give up any sexual relationship with the child's mother. Always providing one still existed. She still had no proof of it.

Recalling the girl in the photograph, she felt no reassurance. Luiz was a lover of beauty in women, and Margarita's looks left nothing to be desired.

She was still standing there under the flow when the cabinet door slid open. Luiz stepped in at her back, hands sliding around her to seek the firm curve of her breasts, lips nuzzling her nape, exposed by the shower cap she was wearing.

'You were gone too long,' he breathed against her skin. 'I could wait no longer for you!' He smoothed a slow passage down the length of her body to seek her inner softness, bringing her to quivering life. 'You fill my every waking thought—even my dreams! No other woman could ever match you!'

If it weren't for the last, she would have succumbed without a struggle. She stiffened in his grasp, fighting the urge to let go with the invective clamouring for release.

'Would it ever occur to you that I might not be in the mood?' she asked with what control she could muster. 'Or is it taken for granted that wives have to be permanently on heat?'

For a moment there was no reaction at all. When he moved it was abruptly, stepping away from her as though he'd been stung. Karen's legs felt weak, her whole body shivery. She'd hit him where it would reckon the most, but there was little satisfaction in it.

He was sitting in a chair wearing a silk robe when

she eventually emerged from the bathroom. He viewed her towelling cover-up with cynical eyes.

'You need have no fear. I've no intention of forcing you into fulfilling your duties.'

'It hadn't occurred to me that you would,' she said. 'I'm entitled to refuse on occasion.'

The muscles around his mouth tautened. 'You're entitled to refuse any time you wish, but there are ways of doing it that—'

'That don't undermine your pride?' Her tone was scathing. 'Why should yours be any more important than mine?'

Regard narrowed, he said softly, 'I think there's more to this than a simple lack of desire. Something happened to you while I was away.'

If ever there was a time, that time was now, but the words wouldn't form.

'Perhaps I just came to my senses at last,' she heard herself saying instead. 'Perhaps I realised that being married to you isn't such a bed of roses after all.'

'I've heard no complaints before this.' The level tone was belied by the glitter in the dark eyes. 'On the contrary, in fact.'

'That was then, this is now.' She was getting in deeper and deeper, yet she couldn't stop herself, the need to hurt paramount. 'I want out!'

Luiz came to his feet in one rapid movement, crossing the room in a stride to take hold of her. The kiss was scorching, his arms like iron bands across her back. Karen staggered a little when he released her.

'There will be no divorce!' he gritted.

'Even if it turned out to be true after all about Lucio Fernandas?' she said with the same heedless compulsion.

The glitter in his eyes became a blaze, smothered in seconds by sheer force of will. 'Even then,' he declared. 'You signed a contract with no escape clause.'

He turned away from her, heading across the room to the communicating door. Karen watched him go in numb acceptance. There was no going back from here. She'd made her decision; now she had to live with it.

Regina seemed to have recovered much of her usual spirits in the morning. The resilience of youth, Karen thought wryly, feeling anything but herself.

Luiz wasn't at breakfast. He'd gone out early, she said when Beatriz asked where he was. The woman suspected something amiss, that was obvious, although she made no comment. Karen would have loved to wipe the smug expression from her face, but it was too late for that.

She went out on to the veranda after the meal. Raymundo followed her, eyeing her with some concern as he took a seat.

'Have you and Luiz had a disagreement?' he asked with a delicacy that might have been amusing in normal circumstances.

'Something like that,' she said. She gave him a smile. 'It will soon blow over.'

He looked unconvinced. 'Luiz can sometimes be a little too assertive, I know.'

Like laying down the law about his own situation, she thought. She opened her mouth to commiserate with him, closing it again with the realisation that what he'd told her about his marriage had been before her memory loss. It was difficult to recall exactly what had happened when. One mistake could expose her.

So what? asked the small voice of reason. Things

could hardly be any worse than they were right now. If nothing else, it would help explain last night's episode.

Why bother? another part of her mind asked. Even if they came to some kind of agreement over Margarita and her son, Luiz would never forgive the things she'd said to him. Like Raymundo himself, she'd made her bed and must lie on it.

'I suppose I'm a bit too assertive myself at times,' she said, trying to inject a touch of humour. 'If Luiz had wanted a wife with no spirit, he would have chosen one,' Raymundo answered. 'He loves you the way you are. I only wish—' He broke off, looking uncomfortable. 'I must be going. I'm sure you will soon be friends again.'

His married life was certainly no bed of roses, Karen reflected as he went back indoors. Beatriz treated him like dirt. His own fault, maybe, but love was notoriously blind in its early stages. She should have remembered that herself.

Luiz didn't come back for lunch either. Karen took the pups for a walk, then retired on the pretext of taking a siesta, though sleeping was the last thing she felt like doing.

She tried to concentrate on a book, but the words made no sense. Eventually, she gave up and just sat there waiting. Luiz had to return some time.

The afternoon was drawing towards evening when he finally put in an appearance. Dressed in his working gear, he came straight to the room she was occupying, face rigid as he regarded her.

'So you had no interest in Villota!' he jerked out. 'Don't try to deny it! You were seen with him in La Santa!'

It had been on the cards, Karen supposed. The possibility had simply been pushed to the back of her mind by everything else.

'I wasn't going to deny it,' she said resignedly. 'We were together no more than fifteen minutes.'

Luiz curled a lip. 'Long enough.'

'Not for what you're thinking.' She came to her feet, shaky but not cowed. 'I was hoping not to have to tell you, but it seems I've no choice. Miran asked me to meet him to talk about Regina. He was afraid she'd taken his interest in her a little too seriously, and didn't know what to do about it.'

Fury leapt in the dark eyes. 'Don't you dare bring Regina's name into this!'

'It's true.' Karen tried to keep her tone level. 'The reason she was so unhappy last night was because Miran had failed to contact her. I thought it best to simply let the whole thing fade away. Miran will be back in São Paulo by now, so she's unlikely to see him again.'

Luiz regarded her with scepticism. 'You expect me to believe you were acting purely in Regina's interests?'

'Not really.' Karen drew a shallow breath, starting to lose her grip. 'You believe me guilty of having the affair with Lucio Fernandas. Why should you trust my word now? I spent several minutes in private conversation with your brother this morning. Perhaps I've designs on him too!'

'That's enough!' Luiz clipped.

'No, it isn't!' She was past caring what she let out. 'If you really want to know why Lucio was on the plane, ask your sister-in-law! Not that I'd expect you to take my word against hers, of course, but if you'd taken the trouble to check your credit card statement for January, you might have seen that I only paid for *one* ticket to Rio, and the same to London. Oh, I saw him on the plane—he was bragging about having lots of money—but he wasn't with me!'

Luiz was gazing at her in dawning realisation. 'You recovered your memory!'

'Every last detail! I suppose I should be flattered that you abandoned your mistress and son to get back to me yesterday—especially when you see so little of them. It's a pity…'

Karen broke off, struck by the expression on the lean, bronzed face.

'My *what*?' he asked.

'It's no use trying to deny it,' she retorted. 'I've seen the photograph you keep in your office drawer. Your son looks just like you!'

'He looks,' Luiz said levelly, 'like my brother Maurice. He was killed in a road accident more than two years ago, before he could put right the wrong he'd done. Margarita mourns him still. She would consider me no substitute.'

Karen swallowed on the dryness in her throat, her mind in turmoil. 'I'm sorry,' she got out. 'I didn't…know.'

'Obviously.' Luiz indicated the chair she'd risen from. 'I think you'd better sit down before you fall down.'

She did so, trying to get her head round it all. 'I don't understand. Beatriz—your mother—they both told me the child was yours.'

'They both lied.' The statement was iron-hard. 'I took over responsibility for Margarita and Maurice as a duty. I visit them when I'm in Brasilia on business, no other time. The photograph was given to me as a mark of gratitude.'

He studied her bewildered face, his own softening a little. 'How long have you been able to remember?'

'Only since yesterday.' She looked at him appealingly. 'What I said to you last night. It wasn't true, any of it. I was eaten up with jealousy. I couldn't stand the thought of sharing you with anyone.'

'I know the feeling,' he said.

'There was no affair. Not with Lucio Fernandas, not with Jorge Arroyo, not with anyone.'

'I believe you.' His tone was wry. 'You were right. If I'd checked the statement it would have proved what you say.' His brows drew together again. 'But that still doesn't explain why you took flight.'

'I'm afraid that was Beatriz too. She showed me the photograph, told me you already had a child. I didn't stop to think things through.'

'You were still suffering the trauma of losing the baby,' he said grimly. 'She will pay dearly for that alone. You believe she paid Fernandas to follow you?'

'She didn't actually deny it when I faced her with it yesterday, just said it would be hard to prove.' Karen made a rueful gesture. 'I let her persuade me that the doubt would still be there in your mind even if I told you I'd got my memory back. I'd almost managed to persuade myself that I could live with things the way they were—until you came to me in the shower. I wanted to hurt you. I wanted to make you feel the way I was feeling. Your pride—'

'Damn my pride!' he said forcefully. 'It was my heart that was shattered! I've never loved any woman before you. I could never think of loving any woman other than you!'

He drew her to her feet again, holding her close, his hands buried in her hair, eyes glowing with an inner fire. 'The moment I saw you, I was lost! I wanted to spend my life with you, to raise a family, to grow old alongside you. I know you don't feel as much for me, but—'

'Perhaps not in the beginning,' she said softly, 'but I do now. I've gone through hell all day thinking about you.' She lifted her hands to his face, tracing the incisive lines with her fingertips. 'It's still hard to believe it's all ended! All the wondering and doubting. I love you so much, Luiz.' She gave a shaky smile. 'Do you think we could go back to where we were last night before I launched that rocket? I've so much to make up for.'

'The fault was never yours,' he said. 'Beatriz is responsible for most of what we've both gone through, but my mother must share the blame.'

He kissed her tenderly on the lips, then put her from him, jaw hardening. 'We'll go back to where we were, never fear, but first I have to deal with my brother and his wife.'

'Raymundo doesn't know what she's been up to,' Karen defended. 'He'll be devastated!'

'He'll be more than that. They'll both of them be gone within the hour, I can promise you!'

'You can't throw your brother out,' she protested as he started for the door. 'He loves Guavada!'

Luiz looked back at her with a frown. 'Are you suggesting I allow Beatriz to get away with what she's done?'

'No.' Karen could say that without hesitation. 'I hate her for it! But let Raymundo stay. He'll be only too happy to be free of her. I know he's been weak—

he knows he's been weak—but give him a chance. There are times when divorce is the only path left to take.'

'There have been times when such a heartfelt plea on behalf of another man—even my own brother—would have been incentive enough to be rid of him,' came the reply after a moment. 'I'll let him decide for himself whether he stays or goes, if it makes you happy.'

'Not just me,' she said. 'You lost one brother, you can't afford to lose another. And Regina needs you both.'

Luiz came back to where she stood to take her in his arms again, lips cherishing hers.

'You are everything a woman should be,' he said gruffly. 'Don't go away.'

Karen had no intention. She watched him go out of the door, loving every masterful, masculine inch of him. She could almost feel sorry for Beatriz, who was going to get the shock of her life. Raymundo would opt to stay, for certain. Eventually he'd meet someone who was right for him.

In the meantime, she and Luiz had a family of their own to build. Starting the moment he returned.

She could hardly wait.

EPILOGUE

'MY WAIST is a whole three inches bigger than it was when I married you,' Karen complained, checking the tape measure.

'One for each baby,' Luiz returned easily. 'Some sacrifices have to be made.'

'And what exactly have *you* sacrificed?' she asked in mock indignation.

He laughed. 'I gave up my freedom for you. The biggest sacrifice a man can make! Are you coming to bed, or do I have to come and fetch you?'

Green eyes sparkled. 'You'll have to catch me first!'

She gave a yelp as he shot from the bed at the speed of lightning to sling her up across his shoulder, pummelling at his bare back with both fists. 'Unfair advantage! I wasn't ready!'

'I am,' he said, dumping her on the pillows.

He wasn't lying. Karen melted beneath him, aroused as always by the muscular strength of him, the oiled smoothness of his skin, the masculine scent. Thirty-eight, and still not one ounce of surplus flesh on his frame.

He took it slowly, making her wait—trailing feathery kisses down over her fluttering stomach muscles to linger for endless, tantalising moments before bestowing the most intimate of kisses. She writhed in ecstasy, fingers tangled in the thicket of black curls.

He never tired of making love to her, never left her

unsatisfied. A man in a million! she told herself eons later in the lazy, hazy aftermath.

Six years! It had passed so fast. Edmundo had been born almost exactly nine months after Beatriz's hasty departure, with Joana eighteen months later, and Maria Teresa just last year. Edmundo looked more and more like his father every day, while the girls took after her. Exactly how it should be, Luiz had declared.

Life couldn't be better than this, Karen thought contentedly. Each and every day she thanked her lucky stars. Without that lottery win, she would never have come to Brazil, never have known Luiz, never have given birth to these three particular children. It had to be kismet!

Luiz had never revealed exactly what passed between him and his sister-in-law that afternoon, but she'd been gone, as he'd promised, within the hour. Raymundo had not been held entirely blameless, but he'd been allowed to stay on at Guavada. The divorce had gone through eventually, though he hadn't found another wife yet. Once bitten, twice shy, Karen supposed.

Regina had been married two years to a man Luiz knew and trusted. No children so far, but there was time. Margarita was married too now, which meant Luiz no longer had sole responsibility for his brother's son, although he still saw the boy when he visited Brasilia.

Although Cristina had claimed sincere remorse for the harm she'd done, Luiz had never really forgiven her. Karen doubted if she and her mother-in-law would ever have a good relationship.

'Not asleep yet?' asked Luiz softly, bringing a smile to her face in the darkness.

'Maybe you could sing me a lullaby,' she said.

He laughed. 'I think I might have a better remedy than that.'

'And you call *me* insatiable,' she accused as he drew her on top of him.

'I thought we might try for another inch on that waistline of yours,' he said. 'Another boy would be nice.'

Karen arched her back, relishing the feel of him deep inside her. Another baby of any description would be nice, she thought happily.

'Perhaps you could manage twins this time,' she said. 'One of each. Five sounds a good number to finish on. On the other hand, all things being equal, we could go for a whole football team. Five a side, girls against boys! Just think of—'

Luiz was laughing; she could feel it right the way through her. He reached up to draw her down to him, cutting off the words with a kiss that drove whatever she had been about to say from her mind.

Not that it mattered.

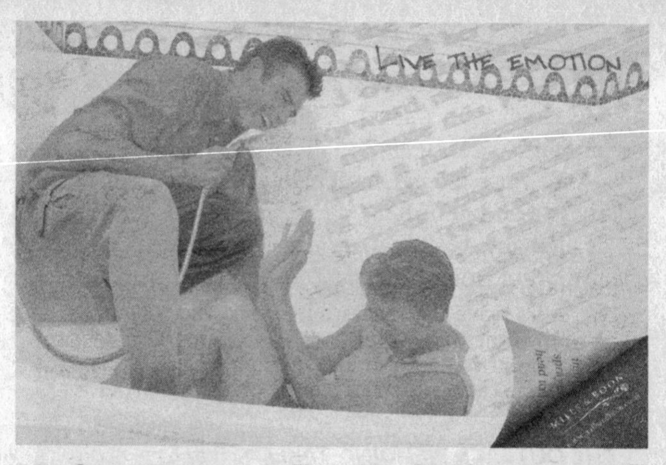

Modern Romance™
...international affairs – seduction and passion guaranteed

Medical Romance™
...pulse-raising romance – heart-racing medical drama

Tender Romance™
...sparkling, emotional, feel-good romance

Sensual Romance™
...teasing, tempting, provocatively playful

Historical Romance™
...rich, vivid and passionate

Blaze Romance™
...scorching hot sexy reads

27 new titles every month.

Live the emotion

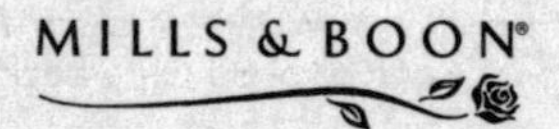

MB4

MILLS & BOON®

Live the emotion

Modern Romance™

THE PASSION BARGAIN *by Michelle Reid*

Italian Carlo Carlucci won't take no for an answer. He has set his sights on Francesca Bernard, who stirs him more than any other woman. But Francesca is engaged to a man Carlo believes is a gold-digger. There's only one way he can protect her – and that's to claim her for himself…

THE OUTBACK WEDDING TAKEOVER *by Emma Darcy*

Mitch Tyler has put his troubled past behind him to become a hot-shot lawyer, and he's the only man who can protect beautiful Kathryn Ledger. Mitch pretends he's just doing his best friend a favour – but he's driven half-crazy by the sexual attraction he has to hide…

MISTRESS AT A PRICE *by Sara Craven*

Cat Adamson is intoxicated by Liam Hargrave and they share an explosive night of passion. She agrees to be his mistress – but that's all. But Liam is a man who always gets what he wants – and he wants Cat! Now she's falling in love – how can Cat change the rules that *she* made…?

THE BILLIONAIRE BODYGUARD *by Sharon Kendrick*

When Keri was stranded with dark, brooding bodyguard Jay Linur, it was clear they were from different worlds. But opposites attract and their passion blew her mind. Keri discovered that Jay was not all he seemed and, though marriage was the last thing he wanted, she found she couldn't walk away…

On sale 4th June 2004

Available at most branches of WHSmith, Tesco, Martins, Borders, Eason, Sainsbury's and all good paperback bookshops.

0504/01a

MILLS & BOON®

Live the emotion

Modern Romance™

THE AUSTRALIAN'S CONVENIENT BRIDE
by Lindsay Armstrong

When Chattie Winslow travels to the Outback to sort out a family drama she isn't expecting to meet handsome Steve Kinane. He needs a housekeeper and she decides to take the job. They try to ignore the intense sexual chemistry between them – but then Steve discovers the real reason Chattie's at Mount Helena...

THE BLACKMAIL PREGNANCY *by Melanie Milburne*

Millionaire Byron Rockcliffe storms back into Cara's life, even though their marriage is long ended. He offers to save her design business from financial ruin, but there's a catch. He's not just looking for an interior designer – he wants Cara to furnish him with a baby...

ONE NIGHT WITH THE TYCOON *by Lee Wilkinson*

When tycoon Graydon Gallagher comforts Rebecca at her ex-fiancé's wedding, she doesn't expect to wake up with him the next day! Gray wants to take her on a business trip, and she has to accept – but the question remains: did they sleep together, or did they *sleep* together...?

THE ITALIAN'S SECRET BABY *by Kim Lawrence*

Scarlet Smith has kept Roman O'Hagan's child a secret from him. The moment he bursts into her life Scarlet recognises the instant electricity between them. But can she keep the truth behind the child's birth a secret...?

On sale 4th June 2004

Available at most branches of WHSmith, Tesco, Martins, Borders, Eason, Sainsbury's and all good paperback bookshops.

0504/01b

Visit millsandboon.co.uk and discover your one-stop shop for romance!

Find out everything you want to know about romance novels in one place. Read about and buy our novels online anytime you want.

- Choose and buy books from an extensive selection of Mills & Boon® titles.
- Enjoy top authors and *New York Times* best-selling authors – from Penny Jordan and Miranda Lee to Sandra Marton and Nicola Cornick!
- Take advantage of our amazing **FREE** book offers.
- In our Authors' area find titles currently available from all your favourite authors.
- Get hooked on one of our fabulous online reads, with new chapters updated weekly.
- Check out the fascinating articles in our magazine section.

Visit us online at

www.millsandboon.co.uk

…you'll want to come back again and again!!

WEB/MB

We would like to take this opportunity to thank you for reading this Mills & Boon® book by offering you the chance to take FOUR more specially selected titles from the Modern Romance™ series absolutely FREE! We're also making this offer to introduce you to the benefits of the Reader Service™—

- ★ FREE home delivery
- ★ FREE gifts and competitions
- ★ FREE monthly Newsletter
- ★ Books available before they're in the shops
- ★ Exclusive Reader Service discount

Accepting these FREE books and gift places you under no obligation to buy; you may cancel at any time, even after receiving your free shipment. Simply complete your details below and return the entire page to the address below. ***You don't even need a stamp!***

YES! Please send me 4 free Modern Romance books and a surprise gift. I understand that unless you hear from me, I will receive 6 superb new titles every month for just £2.69 each, postage and packing free. I am under no obligation to purchase any books and may cancel my subscription at any time. The free books and gift will be mine to keep in any case.

P4ZEE

Ms/Mrs/Miss/Mr ....Initials...

BLOCK CAPITALS PLEASE

Surname...

Address..

....

....Postcode ....

Send this whole page to:
UK: The Reader Service, FREEPOST CN81, Croydon, CR9 3WZ
EIRE: The Reader Service, PO Box 4546, Kilcock, County Kildare (stamp required)

Offer not valid to current Reader Service subscribers to this series. We reserve the right to refuse an application and applicants must be aged 18 years or over. Only one application per household. Terms and prices subject to change without notice. Offer expires 29th August 2004. As a result of this application, you may receive offers from Harlequin Mills & Boon and other carefully selected companies. If you would prefer not to share in this opportunity please write to The Data Manager at PO Box 676, Richmond TW9 1WU.

Mills & Boon® is a registered trademark owned by Harlequin Mills & Boon Limited.
Modern Romance™ is being used as a trademark.
The Reader Service™ is being used as a trademark.